W9-BDY-776

SPACE PRECINCT

Based on the popular new television series, *Space Precinct* novels follow a tough, street-smart New York cop to the far corners of the galaxy.

Veteran NYPD Lieutenant Patrick Brogan drew a wild card in the intergalactic Law Enforcement Exchange program. He has moved his entire family, including his ten-year-old daughter Liz and his teenage son Matt, to the planet Altor.

There are problems enough for a new family in Altor's orbiting "space suburbs." But Brogan's toughest job is down below, in the high-tech slums of Demeter City, where alien species from all over the galaxy—each with its own crime speciality—meet in a melting pot of mayhem and murder!

Dear Reader:

Just a moment of your time could earn you $1,000! We're working hard to bring you the best books, and to continue to do that we need your help. Simply turn to the back of this book, and let us know what you think by answering seven important questions.

Return the completed survey with your name and address filled in, and you will automatically be entered in a drawing to win $1,000, subject to the official rules.

Good luck!

Geoff Hannell
Publisher

Gerry Anderson's
SPACE PRECINCT

The Deity-Father
Demon Wing
Alien Island*

From HarperPrism

**coming soon*

ATTENTION: ORGANIZATIONS AND CORPORATIONS

Most HarperPaperbacks are available at special quantity discounts for bulk purchases for sales promotions, premiums, or fundraising. For information, please call or write:

Special Markets Department, HarperCollins*Publishers*,
10 East 53rd Street, New York, N.Y. 10022.
Telephone: (212) 207-7528. Fax: (212) 207-7222.

Gerry Anderson's

SPACE PRECINCT

• DEMON WING •

DAVID BISCHOFF

HarperPrism
An Imprint of HarperPaperbacks

If you purchased this book without a cover, you should be aware that this book is stolen property. It was reported as "unsold and destroyed" to the publisher and neither the author nor the publisher has received any payment for this "stripped book."

This is a work of fiction. The charcaters, incidents, and dialogues are products of the author's imagination and are not to be construed as real. Any resemblence to actual events or persons, living or dead, is entirely coincidental.

HarperPaperbacks *A Division of* HarperCollins*Publishers*
10 East 53rd Street, New York, N.Y. 10022

Copyright © 1995 by Grove Television Enterprises
All rights reserved. No part of this book may be used or reproduced in any manner whatsoever without written permission of the publisher, except in the case of brief quotations embodied in critical articles and reviews. For information address HaperCollins*Publishers*, 10 East 53rd Street, New York, NY 10022.

Cover illustration © 1995 by Grove Television Enterprises

First printing: September 1995

Printed in the United States of America

HarperPrism is an imprint of HarperPaperbacks. HarperPaperbacks, HarperPrism, and colophon are trademarks of HarperCollins*Publishers*

❖ 10 9 8 7 6 5 4 3 2 1

To Jimmy Vines

SPACE PRECINCT

◆ DEMON WING ◆

PROLOGUE

Above the Demeter skyline, struggling through the haze of pollution and the occasional tendril of fog, hard stars shone down like the eyes of a malevolent night.

Tark Norgal slunk through the alley, clutching the bundle to his chest. It wiggled and sobbed softly against him, smelling of damp and fear. As he slunk along, the Creon trod through foul papers and tossed bottles, and the tintinnabulation of echoes made a kind of eerie night music to this unsacred *hegira.* There was a bitter taste in his mouth that had nothing to do with the murk-wine he'd downed instead of dinner tonight, nor the moth-liquor in his flask that he'd nip at against the cold of the niche-fog, and to fortify his dwindling courage.

Normally, Tark was not the sort of Creon who indulged in this kind of thing. No, not at all. He was by day an upstanding merchant with a respectable corner grocery and food stand that did good business—that was, until the neighborhood of the Brox went to seed, and his respectable, moneyed customers moved away. The sort of folk who replaced them shoplifted far more than they bought, bringing trouble upon a previously prosperous store and personal life.

Alas, Tark could find no buyers for his business, but his bachelor life was tied to it. He did not know what to do. . . .

And then, one day, a Tarn wearing a black robe and silver sash entered his store, to the accompaniment of the twiddle-bell signal attached to the jamb. . . .

A swirl of mist unwound in front of him, caressing his face with cool and shivers. A distant bell near the docks had long since rung off an hour deep past midst-night. Although occasional street-lamps were stationed along the alleyway systems, and windows of various buildings leaked illumination like misers, the shadows were thicker than the bright, and the colors here were all in shades of grim and dim. Although he'd brought along a glow-light, he did not want to turn it on as yet.

There were predators in the mist.

It made no sense to light up an arrow to himself when he could make his way along a wall, trippingly to be sure, but adequately. A shame the Elders had appointed the spot they had for the Relinquishing. Of course, they'd claimed they had no choice. The auguring and the sewer-flow charts had portended this to be the time, this to be the spot.

To obtain what he desired above all else, he would have to play by what They decreed.

The Creon heard the Dialogue echo in his mind.

Are you not a faithful Acolyte?

Yes, Brother.

Is there not Power upon the face of the Night?

Yes, Brother.

Do you not wish to Taste of that Power?

Yes, Brother.

Behold. Here are the Charts.

Yes, Brother.

Take the prescribed Token to be Offered. And yea—your reward shall be great, and the Appeasement will profit us all.

Yes, Brother.

And, dear Tark—remember . . . Do not look full upon the Fiery Face, lest your eyes liquefy and drip down your cheeks.

Yes, Brother.

At the memory of those words, a shudder racked the Creon's big-boned body.

He was no larger than any other Creon on Demeter City, or, for that matter, the Home Planet of Danae; nor was he much smaller. His frame was distinctly humanoid. Two legs, two arms, with two hands holding fingers and opposable thumbs. However, his head, although it had two eyes, a nose, and a mouth, was humanoid in only the vaguest of senses. It was ruddy and wrinkled, this face, with a tuft of wirelike hair. The two eyes seemed eager to be as far apart from each other as possible. They were binocular-like things set atop large ridges of bone and flesh in a manner aesthetic only to other Creons. Targ had been a little more burly in his wealthier days, but he was by no means slender now. Beneath the cloak, he wore the usual Creon worker outfit—gray coveralls.

Thus, he was now simply a nondescript citizen, slinking through back alleys, holding a lumpy, moving sack!

What could be more normal?

He paused for a moment, took a mouthful of harsh liquor, grimaced. Ah, the ways of his ancestors in the peat marshes of Danae were primitive but effective. The alcohol sang a song of blissful oblivion in his veins. He blinked his watering eyes, belched, grabbed a better hold of his burden, and then stumped onward into the mysterious night.

The liquor cut down some of the stench here as well: an unpleasant miasma of garbage, offal, decay, with a hint of less pleasant things. The bitter taste of the drink cut down on the bitter taste in his heart.

He kept his goal in mind as he cut through the mist.

Power.

Money.

And, for once, *luck*.

Who would begrudge an aging bachelor these things? Desperation drove him to these measures, and surely the Universe would understand.

And the Being he courted would grant him what he wished.

He crossed a cobblestone way, turned a corner.

Denser, swirling fog confronted him.

Something squeaked and skittered under his feet.

Ah well.

This was the place—the Courtyard of Joy.

At one time, at the beginning of Demeter City history, this place had been an open market of activity. Children had played here, and people had intermingled and conversed.

Now, it was an intersection of loss. Benches were upturned. Piles of refuse lay moldering in corners. Children's playground items lay wrecked and twisted. The stench was overpowering.

Tark took another swig of moth-liquor from his flask, squinted through the swirling fog.

There it was, sticking up from the ground, gray and cement and blocky.

The altar.

This was where his offering would commence. His sacrifice to Sugath.

Upon this cracked, old altar.

In truth, the thing had not been designed as such. Once it had been the podium for a statue. Now, though, the statue had been pushed down and its pieces either carted off or become part of the rubble that filled the area. However, for nights such as these, dark and nasty and filled with portent, for some reason the place attracted the energy currents that the Elders were able to map, and served quite well as an altar.

Tark approached it carefully, looking left and right for any signs of watchers.

No one.

He advanced warily, then placed the cloth-wrapped thing he carried upon the "altar." Taking pains, he brought out his org-light, turned it on. It created a strange, cold glow atop the squarish mound of concrete. Just strong enough to work by.

The cloth mound quivered.

Targ unfastened pins. He peeled back the cloth.

Uncovered the thing within.

It was a small animal, a *marga*-beast. He'd anesthetized it earlier, after he'd bought it from an underworld figure who traded in such rare creatures. Now, it was semiconscious, and it quivered as though experiencing paroxysms of dreams. A quadruped, it might be said by an Earthperson that it looked like a lumpy dog. It had buggy eyes and a narrow mouth, through which protruded sharp fangs. A light, leathery armor covered its hairless skin.

It was a carnivore and a dangerous creature.

The dealer had assured him that the injection of mong-leaf essence would keep it semicomatose for as long as necessary. There was no reason to disbelieve him.

Tark pushed his hands into his pockets again, brought out a crimson crystal set upon a tripod.

He stroked a button.

The crystal began to throb with a milky, ethereal light. A soft, barely perceptible keening sounded.

Targ breathed a sigh, and then he pulled the large, ceremonial knife from its sheath at his belt. The razor-sharp edge glittered in the murky twin lights on the altar.

The *marga*-beast squeaked in its sleep as though sensing danger.

Lifting the knife up in the air, Tark began to chant the alien words that the Elders had taught him.

The chant blended into the keen from the singing jewel, making a queer, shivery chorus that blended into the mist and the shadows like an unholy invocation.

For a moment, all was silence.

Then, distantly . . . something.

Tark shivered with anticipation. He strained his eyes. Strained all his senses. A *shushing* sound, almost familiar . . .

Then he recognized it.

Traffic.

Distant traffic, that was all.

He felt disappointed. He relaxed somewhat and took a deep breath. The sacrificial beast stirred slightly, yet was still held in its drug bonds.

Best to proceed with the killing to attract the demigod.

He raised the knife higher and began to chant the words in which he had been instructed, ending with ". . . and bring to me the powers that imbue your magnificence, that prosperity may come to yours truly, your servant . . . and those that hallow thy name."

The beast below growled.

Best to be done with this, he thought, and he moved his arms to bring the knife down to slash the life out of the innocent, to burst the blood vessels, to send its soul sailing out as an offering to the hungry prowler in the night. . . .

However, the knife seemed stuck.

Something had wrapped around his wrists, restraining him, preventing him from bringing his weapon down to kill the creature. Targ looked around and up . . .

And gasped.

He had not seen or sensed its approach, but there it was . . . huge and overwhelming, half thundercloud, half ghost. Somehow simultaneously material and immaterial, wisps of might, spirit, and energy reaching out in streamers, streaked with lightning.

Sugath!

The demigod!

Desperation drove the words past his terror.

"Sugath! Allow me to give you my offering."

The creature rippled with thunder, echoing into another dimension. There was a diaphanous terror raging over it, and it seemed veined with the very energies of the cosmos.

Below him, on the altar, the *marga*-beast awoke, and stood up. It stared, angrily at Targ, baring its sharp fangs, its claws growing.

No! This was not supposed to happen this way.

He was not supposed to be the sacrifice.

However, the *marga*-beast thought differently, leaping for the Creon's face, as the demigod settled down to suck out his spirit.

CHAPTER 1

Lieutenant Patrick Brogan had seen dead things before.

Dead humans, dead animals, dead aliens . . .

Deadbeats.

When you were a cop, you saw plenty of things you didn't particularly want to see.

He'd never seen anything quite like this dead thing before, though, not through forty-some years of life, not through twenty-some years on the Force.

"I put the scan through Central," said Officer Jack Haldane, looking up from his Porta-Pad.

"You get the DNA and retinal scan?" asked Brogan tersely.

"The DNA. Retinal's iffy. Not much left of the eyes, I'm afraid."

"I think I noticed."

"So far sensors indicate that what we've got here, Lieutenant, is one Creon. One important thing about this Creon, Lieutenant?"

"Yeah?"

"Yeah. It's dead."

"The Creon part's good information to know. I think I had a very strong hunch about the dead part, though."

Demeter City's sun struggled through greenish clouds and polluted murk to shed some light on this alley scene. The area was still drenched in shadows, outlined in trash cans and refuse, with that funky old smell that New York City and other grim cities owned as well, with a little exotic alien "P.U." thrown in for spice.

A couple of backup cruisers had swooped down and cordoned off the area with CRIME SCENE signs and bright yellow zap fields. But that didn't stop the gawkers. Lowlifes of every persuasion had noticed the ruckus and were now peering, pink-eyed, big-eyed, or multi-eyed into the scene. Brogan was ranking officer so he got the treat of picking over the corpse before the morgue unit showed.

Gray and sepia, black and odd were the colors of the moment—along with the curious greenish-tinged crimson that was Creon blood.

It looked as though some mad painter had dipped his brush into a bucket of the stuff, and then gone completely wild over the landscape.

Some of it had collected in pools, but for the most part the Creon's blood had been splattered about as though he'd been turned into a grass spray, twirling and spewing for a long time. Brogan wondered if there was anything left in the body.

Or rather, the *pieces* of the body.

Unfortunately, Brogan had seen cut-up bodies before. When you were in Homicide for a while, you saw a lot of nasty stuff.

However, what he'd never seen before was what had *happened* to the body pieces. It looked not only as though they'd been ripped and chewed apart—but then drained and withered of some vital stuff other than blood.

"Creon jerky," said Haldane.

"What an appetizing thought. Accurate but unfortunate."

"Yeah. I used to like jerky, too."

The Porta-Pad blinked and spluttered. Information threaded over its screen and lights blinked.

"I think it wants to tell you something," said Brogan.

"Hmm. . . . You know it would have been a lot easier if this dude had been toting his driver's license."

"DNA's a lot harder to fake."

"Too true." The good-looking young officer scrooched his face up as he scrutinized the instrument. "Ah yes. It looks as though who we have here is one Targ Nargal of Mixdao District. A businessman, it would seem. Respected, but according to his tax returns, fallen upon hard times. Time of death—looks like about three-fifteen in the morning."

"Question is, what was he doing in the Mixdao District?"

"What is *anyone* doing in the Mixdao District? Anyone but pushers and thieves and drunken idiots who don't know better. This guy was supposed to be a respected citizen." A little light shivered on the screen. "Hold it a moment. The comps have got their teeth into something. They're working it hard—real hard. . . ."

It looked as though something *else* had sunk its teeth in this Targ guy, thought Brogan as he examined a good-sized chunk of leg. Something with sharp and jagged teeth. A carnivore, certainly, and bestial, and yet he could see no sign that any of the Creon had actually been eaten.

But then who, after all, would want to eat a Creon?

"Hoo boy," said Haldane.

"What do you have?"

"Plenty. According to Intelligence, there's every reason to believe that Mister Targ here was involved with some kind of weird cult."

"Oh. Great. Cults. My favorite."

"It's doing a search. I'll give you more later."

Brogan looked up, shielding his eyes. "I don't think we'll have to wait. I think we've got a fount of information descending upon us at this very moment."

Coming down was a large hopper with quite official-looking insignia and big fins.

It landed in a clear area, dusting away newspapers and detritus with its jets.

A door opened, a loud growl boomed from the cab, and a large ungainly figure brought a scowl out of the car, and pushed it forward on a pair of sturdy legs and a face that only a mother or another Creon could love.

"Brogan! Haldane!" called Captain Podly gruffly. "Stand aside. I need a look."

"Oh, help yourself!" said Haldane. "There's plenty to look at, that's for sure."

"Levity has its place, m'lad," said the bulky alien with the ranking insignia on his regulation black leather jacket. He grimly clumped up beside them. "Not at a murder scene, though. You hear me?"

Those odd, protuberant Creon eyes amid that wrinkled face swung around aggressively. Podly made absolutely no bones about making sure everyone knew who was in charge.

"Yes, sir," said Haldane. He sneaked a queasy look at Brogan.

Patrick Brogan nodded. He felt sorry for his partner. Jack had been a cop for only a few years. He didn't have the crust you got after years of corpses. Hell, you never got used to it, that was for sure—but when you were just starting out, about all you had between keeping a handle on things and heading for the nearest john and hurling was a cocky attitude and stupid jokes. Brogan always thought it would be easier to look at an alien corpse. But after getting to know aliens, be they Tarns or Creons or whatever, he realized they were living, sentient beings and be it green blood or red blood, you had to cope with that sense of your own mortality nonetheless.

Podly took in the scene with focused scrutiny. Those big eyes missed nothing, Brogan knew.

Those large nostrils quivered, seemed to suck in sensory data even a keen police officer like Brogan wasn't aware of.

"I was down talking to the city council," Podly barked in his Creon regional accent, which sounded amazingly Irish. "The report of this murder came over the honker. With the other killings, I figured it would be judicious to come down. I see I was right."

A little more pacing. A little more sniffling.

Then Podly nodded. He turned to Haldane. "What do you have there, son?"

Haldane looked down at the pad and began to read off information.

"Here. Give it to me," said the Creon. Impatiently, he grabbed the pad, glanced at it, then furiously punched in some further requests.

Fuming, he read the results.

He sighed.

Brogan wasn't sure what alien protocol was for these matters. Back home, though, you just waited for as long as it took for the captain to drop the other shoe. All in all, that recourse seemed to be the wise one now.

Eventually, though, Podly came up out of his funk for some air.

"Aye! Faith, it's happened again."

Brogan nodded. That was his analysis as well. That was what Haldane should have told Podly. That was the implicit question the Creon was asking. Is this another of the bizarre serial killings that had been happening?

He wondered if Haldane had figured that too, but was just trying to make sure he wasn't jumping to any conclusions.

"This is not good. I trust you told the other officers to keep the media away?"

"They're doing their best. I just wish that morgue wagon and forensic team would hurry up and get here so this place can get cleared out."

Podly looked around.

"Gentleman. Wrap this up and bring me the relevant data. There are things I can't say out in the open." He made a face as though he smelled something very bad, which, down here in the Mixdao District, was highly likely. "And even back at the precinct I'm going to need a privacy shield." He brusquely handed the pad back to Haldane.

"We'll be back in two hours, Chief," said Brogan.

"Make it an hour and a half, you two. Show me what you Earth people are made of." He grunted, then stalked back to his waiting car with no further niceties.

"You know, Haldane," said Brogan, "I've got a feeling that my weekend has just been shot all to hell."

Haldane did not joke back. "Well mine better not be!" he said, eyes blazing. "I've got plans. . . . *Serious* plans!"

Haldane went back to deal with the other cops, leaving Brogan wondering what the hell was going on.

Then he remembered.

Despite the gore and grief that lay strewn all about, he smiled.

CHAPTER 2

Necessity Number One:

A cup of coffee.

Patrick Brogan let out a deep sigh and leaned against the beverage dispenser. He tapped up a display on the screen, rubbed his bleary eyes. Dammit, he was tired. He'd been up since before the crack of dawn and he was feeling it. He didn't feel like dealing with screen lettering. However, he was never too tired to take another stab at something that was this important to him.

He hit a button that changed things to audio.

What he would take from the dispenser was a cup of coffee.

What he really wanted, though, was a cup of *good* coffee.

"Good morning, Mister Patrick Brogan," said the machine. "How may I be of service?"

"Hi, Bev." He was the only one who called the

machine Bev. It didn't seem to mind one way or the other. "Thought I'd give it another shot."

"Excellent. I am programmed to please."

"I don't suppose the forensic chemists have programmed anything new into your systems."

"No."

"Yeah. Well, I haven't gotten anything from Earth yet. I guess they just haven't got the right contacts."

"It would seem to be easy enough to ship some coffee beans here."

"I suppose they'll get around to it eventually. I guess they just don't see it as a real priority at the moment."

"A shame."

"Yes. Well, I don't feel like looking at tables. Last time wasn't right, but it was off only in the taste and the body . . ."

"You spit out the first swallow, as I recall."

"Yeah, it was bad at first. But I got used to it quick. The caffeine content is just fine. That's why I struggle through it all the time, Bev. Need the jolt."

"According to recently memory files, caffeine is not particularly good for your species, Mister Patrick Brogan. May I suggest a nice glass of pine-orange juice, synthesized from a splendid sample imported from New Hawaii?"

"Bev, you've been trying to foist that stuff on me since I got here. I like it fine. But it's not coffee. I'm a New York cop, Bev. I need my joe, my java, my steaming cup of coffee. Got it? Good. Now let's have another shot at it."

Quickly he gave another stab at the necessary formula, altering acidity and adding alkaline. A little more flavoids?

A pinch. He remembered the way that last cup tasted, then added a few more pinches.

There were other elements and he played with those.

The milk part wasn't hard, or the sugar. He could live with the variations he got on those here. It was just the damned coffee part. Because shipping and trading weren't quite on-line with Earth, everything from Earth had be synthesized. Matt, his teenage son, was still miffed he couldn't get Coca-Cola that tasted like real Coke. Nor was Liz, his eleven-year-old daughter, exactly thrilled that Kool-Aid and Twinkies weren't exactly the same. But then, that was all junk food.

This was *coffee*, dammit.

A cop needed *coffee*.

He'd kinda maybe figured out something drinkable back home on his machine, but that had been hit-or-miss.

Things were still dicey here, particularly with such a 'helpful' program so very eager to help him.

He punched in the final variations on the chemical makeup, then hit the PRODUCE button.

Deep in the electromag-whosit/whatsit of the machine, bowels gurgled and engines whirred. There was a questioning whine, a pause . . .

A "plink."

Quickly Brogan put his prize coffee mug—labeled NYPD ALLSTARS—underneath the nozzle of the dispenser. Within moments, an uneasy brownish muddy mixture splashed out into the mug, building up a frothy whitish head. Brogan, as always, prayed for the aroma of fresh-ground arabica beans. What he got was something a little more like old underwear.

Hesitantly, he blew on the mixture.

Sipped.

He grimaced.

Awful. Old shoe leather laced with caffeine. Yikes! He really had to get together with a chemist somewhere . . .

Another sip . . . and he realized he'd put too much of everything in it—but hell, it was drinkable, he supposed. Better luck next time.

He walked toward his appointed meeting with Podly. A good cup of coffee would have gone a long way toward making all this horror that had been going on a little easier to swallow. He could tell he was probably going to need a stomach antacid after this baby, but when you needed caffeine, you needed caffeine. . . .

"Hey, Brogan," said Sergeant Orrinn, as he walked into the main headquarters room. The thin Creon with the fuzzy red hair was bending over, conferring with Slomo, the station mobile 'bot.

"C'mere a minute, will ya?"

Brogan looked at his wristwatch. "Sure, but just a minute, okay? Podly's gonna have my butt for breakfast if I'm late for this one."

"Yeah, I hear this serial killer stuff's a lulu," said the Creon. "Hope I can help out, but seein' as

I'm mostly a desk jockey. . . . Well, you need help up here with any paper pushing, you just ask your old bud Orrinn. Tell you what, though. I'm having a little difference of opinion with this bucket of bolts here. I thought, you being from a backward planet and all, you might be able to resolve it."

"Backward planets can help resolve differences?"

"Yeah. It's a fact. You get a planet with a lot of factions like yours, you Earthers got some good arbitration skills."

"Glad to know it. Hi, Slomo."

The bulky and round machine's saucer head whirred about, its oculars swiveling toward Brogan. Lights blinked in agreeable colors. "Good day, Lieutenant Brogan. In your vernacular, how is it going?"

"Well, just saw a dead Creon, cut into pieces. His blood was used as a new coat of paint for a bad section of town. I'm headed for a another loud conference with Captain Podly, and this coffee I just made is the pits. So, I guess you'd say, it's business as usual, Slomo."

"Okey-dokey, Lieutenant Brogan. You have a nice day!" said the robot.

"You know, I appreciate the extra work you all have made to make us Earthers feel welcome here. . . ." said Brogan. "Just don't put any smiley faces on Slomo here, okay?"

"Sure, Brogan. Whatever those are . . . so here's the problem. I got a hundred-credit bet with this metallurgy mutant here. Basically, I say that Officers Castle and Haldane got something going . . .

you know, romantically. I'm betting they're sharing toothbrushes within the year!"

The robot's lights blinked frantically. "Negative. I have distinctly heard words of explicit hatred and dispassion exchanged between the young Earth people. True, they are heterosexuals, and true, they are young. Medical records show they contain more estrogen and testosterone than the average humans of their age. They are both of above-average human aesthetic qualities and display sexual qualities which can only be titled vernacularly in human terms."

"And what's that term, pal?" said Orrinn, smugly.

"'Cute.'"

"You see! So me, I've been watching those two. Being a Creon and all, I know a thing or two about love and sex, you betcha, yes sirree Bob! And I'm telling you, I think we're going to be hearing stump thunks and bone cracks within two years?"

"Stump thunks and bone cracks?" said Brogan.

"The Creon equivalent to your culture's 'wedding bells,' I believe," said Slomo in his strange combination of monotone and expressiveness.

"What's your take on this, Slomo?" said Brogan, angling for a little time so he'd know what to say.

"I have studied your Earth cultures somewhat," said the robot. "The American and English cultures represented are from the same roots. Courting is generally a pleasant if precarious affair before mating. Flowers and candy and such, according to my data. I detect much anger and frustration in

Officer Haldane's attitude, not commensurate with courting ritual. I also detect a great deal of emotional coldness in Officer Castle. Most certainly Officer Haldane's reaction is a more rapid heartbeat in the presence of Officer Castle. However, that reaction ceases after suggestive propositions of romantic trysts are met with the representative phrase, 'In your dreams, Haldane.'"

Orrinn slapped his hand against his face and dragged it down wearily. "Slomo, Slomo . . . The data may be correct, but your interpretation is wrong. Like take an old Creon spooning ritual back on our homeworld of Danae. We call it bog bobbing. A girl likes a guy, and they're close to a natural resource. The girl pushes the guy into a bog. What can I say? It's love! They're generally painting the town and screaming at one another." Orrinn scratched his Brillo pad of hair. "You humans may have funny-looking eyes and may be ugly as sin, but I see a lot of similarities. Me, I'm lookin' forward to using my hundred credits on something very special."

"I believe if I had emotions, I would be annoyed at your foolish bravado," said Slomo, in a way that could almost be called peevish.

Brogan took a sip of his bad coffee and sighed. "Guys, guys, I don't know why you made this bet. Who the heck can really figure those two out? Sometimes I think they're nuts about each other, and sometimes I want to tell Podly to put them in corners. I'll tell you one thing about human behavior. Sometimes you just can't predict it. Me, I'd guess that bet could go either way—and you both are going to have a suspenseful time."

"Warning," said Slomo. "Subjects of discussion entering room and headed our way."

Orrinn looked flummoxed. "Hope they didn't hear us. You see. They look unhappy with each other. They could already be *married* by that sign!"

The young duo looked distinctly unhappy with one another.

"So you'll come then," said Haldane.

"Yes. Of course. I've always wanted to go, Haldane," said the auburn, vivacious—and now, clearly vexed Jane Castle. As always, Brogan was struck not only by her slim yet superbly feminine figure, but with her fresh good looks. Even frowning—as she was now—she was a remarkably attractive young woman. "Took's been talking about it for ages. I didn't know I'd be forced to sit with you!"

"Look, I did you a favor, okay? I'll be at your place at seven-thirty tonight. Relax. We're going to have a great time!"

Castle raised a suspicious eyebrow at her walking companion, then turned and acknowledged Brogan, Orrinn, and Slomo. She smiled charmingly. Even Slomo looked as though he was about to melt into a pool of slag. "Forgive us. I appear to have been corralled into attending a special Tarn Ceremony in the company of one of your fellow officers. However, I should like to make it plain—this is not a date!"

Orrinn whispered to Slomo. "I hope they'll name their firstborn after me!"

"Nonsense," said the robot, his lights blinking erratically.

"Well, hope you have a good time," said Brogan. "However, right now we'd better get to a certain Captain Podly's office very quickly or fur will fly!"

"Slomo, why didn't *you* get me tickets?" asked Castle as the trio headed for Podly's area. "I'd far rather have gone with someone with personality and charm!"

Slomo's lights merely blinked a deep blushing pink.

In his designated area, Captain Podly, chief of this Space Precinct, was engrossed in a computer printout. Podly seemed to have extra senses, though—he always seemed to know exactly what was going on everywhere even while he sat behind his desk. Like a spider at the center of its web, thought Brogan. Only the flies had to come to it to get their heads chewed off.

He was eating a sandwich. Little webbed feet were sticking out from beneath the orange bread and purple sauce. Podly took a bite. Snap and crunch. A webbed foot disappeared into the maw beneath his swollen, craggy head.

"Have a seat, people. I'll be with you in a moment. I'm just swallowing some data here."

And God knew what else, thought Brogan to himself grimly as he put his cup of bad coffee down on the desk. Any inquiry into Creon eating habits usually made his stomach turn worse than his commissary-machine experiments at coffee.

Castle made sure that Brogan was between her

and Haldane, to the young man's chagrin. Just as well. They were going to have to start concentrating on some serious and deadly business.

"Just got the forensic lab reports in on the most recent body," said Podly, launching right into the matter. "The details are precisely the same as the other six victims in the past month. Body was literally ripped to pieces. Those pieces charred. And new data here . . . There's always been missing neurological chemicals, but more to the point it would appear that just before the victims were decapitated, charred, and ripped apart, their electrochemical systems were literally sucked dry as a bonglizard sucks out a titanbug."

"Like a vampire sucking energy," said Brogan, nodding. "I was wondering about that from the other reports.

"An electromagnetic Dracula?" said Castle.

"I vant to bite your nerves!" said Haldane in a Transylvanian accent.

"Earth literary/cinema legend," explained Castle.

"Couched in whatever terms, this is death, people. Death is universal, wherever there's life. It's okay if it happens normally. However, if it doesn't, if murder and killing are involved—Well, people that's our job. Death is serious business, and we've got a killer down there. . . . And it's a killer the likes of whom I, for one, have never experienced." Podly shook his head sadly.

There was a moment of uncomfortable silence.

The thing about Podly that made you forgive the crusty exterior was the depth of his being. Captain

Podly *cared.* He cared about his people. He cared about the Force as a whole. But most of all, he cared about Demeter City and its citizens, be they Creon or Tarn or human—or Slugdrips from Altair IV. Podly believed that if you were sentient and abided by the law, you had the right to a good life, a right to be protected. This was part of a code, part of a strong philosophy that kept him going in his position, at the heart of a very difficult job.

"We've got to stop it," said Castle, echoing his concern.

"Not just our duty," echoed Haldane. "But our calling. Put us on it, sir. We'll do it."

Brogan nodded. "Well, we'll do our best, anyway."

"That's why you're here, you three. You're some of the best, the cream from Earth—you come from a good crime-fighting system, and you're good, principled cops." Podly patted the printout with his thick hand. "I'm going to have copies of this information printed out for all of you. Tomorrow you all have the day off. What I'll be asking you to do is to go over it. There's a lot of information here. I can't put it all together. There may be things you see that neither I nor computer analysis—also supplied—sees." Podly stood up, stretched. "That's another reason why you three are here. You know that?"

Why? thought Brogan. *Because we're willing to do homework?*

Haldane looked relieved, though. Obviously he still had the night off. Castle merely looked professional and attentive. "I think, sir, that we all scored high on intuitive levels."

"Absolutely, Castle. You humans may have very low telepathic abilities, just like we Creons do. But no Tarns I've ever encountered had hunches like you do. You take an experienced cop from Earth, you put him in a situation—and you'll get a response not just from reason, but from something else . . . call it intuitive if you like, call it just plain hard-boiled cop sense. What it does is go where high-tech doesn't. So read these over. See what you think."

"Yes, sir," said Brogan.

"And Monday, I'm going to need a little bit of investigation, I think. Brogan, Haldane—we've already deduced that this Targ fellow that was killed last night was involved with a cult. We're short on information on this cult. I want you to go down and see what you can dig up on it on the streets." He opened the sheaf of papers, tapped a page with a ragged fingernail. "I've got some leads listed here. Check 'em out Monday."

Brogan was grateful that Podly used Earth nomenclature to talk about days. He didn't know what he'd do without Sundays.

They all took their stacks of papers. "Yes, sir, we'll be all bright-eyed and bushy-tailed on Monday morning!"

"That will be an interesting look for humans," grunted the Creon. He leaned forward, looking intense. "Help me get this murderer, people. This is bigger than it looks. It gives me the shivers."

"You care to elaborate on that, sir?"

Podly's big eyes looked a little haunted. "Not right now. Only if necessary. Let's just say it's got something to do with a Danaein legend and when something like this happens, someone's doing something unpleasant on my burial tree."

They all gave appropriate glum looks in response, which seemed to gratify the Creon. He went back to his sandwich and his macabre reading.

On the way out, Castle gave Brogan a dirty look. "Speak for yourself on that bright-eyed and bushy-tailed business, Lieutenant," she said. "I've got one of the labors of Hercules this weekend."

"A date that's not a date!" said Haldane. "Sounds pretty tough, huh? A handsome escort to a privileged affair. Maybe a cordial drink afterward. Some stimulating conversation. A safe ushering home. Then a peck on the cheek—*if* she's lucky."

Castle gave a wry look. "See what I mean?"

Brogan chuckled. "Have fun, kids. I'm outta here. I got my paperback reading for the weekend." He held up his printout.

They went their own ways.

On his way to the bathroom, Haldane was stopped in the hallway by Orrinn. "Well, Brogan. Watcha say? I'm a shoo-in for a hot hundred gees, huh?"

Brogan shook his head. "Orrinn, good buddy, I wouldn't bet anything on *that* pair."

The fuzzy-haired Creon looked befuddled as Brogan went past him to dump what was left of his 'coffee' into an unfortunate sink.

CHAPTER 3

Hate.

Confusion.

Anger.

Senselessness.

Above the nighttime spears of Demeter City, shafted into the starry sky, the wisps of fog, the creature floats.

Like a shroud, with its gossamer-thin strands, it spreads itself among the dirty roofs, through alleyways. Its tendrils are like the least visible of mists, and its core itself is kilometers wide, molecule-thin.

Occasionally, energy crackles along its faerie-wing nervous system, making the hackles of some Creon stand up, or causing a shiver to rise up the spine of a Tarn—or make the odd human wish he'd never ventured beyond his homeworld.

The thing ventures. It seeks what it needs.

It is hungry.

This is the one fact that it knows, the one essential detail with which it is consumed throughout the skein of its existence. The previous night it had fed, but the energies it had received were paltry, negative. Now, the black bits of its energyshroud are darker yet.

It seeks out the perfect energy source, the exact biofield that will give it not only sustenance, but meaning.

Thus, winging over Demeter City, this creature from beyond these *stars flaps and stalks.*

A tendril touches a cleaner neighborhood. An area of marble buildings, proud architecture. Music and scents and something far more alluring stream from this.

Undulating in this direction like an octopus scuttling over the dark floor of some exotic sea, the creature streams toward the hall of music.

Hunger fills it.

And an emptiness far deeper.

CHAPTER 4

"I just want you to be *very* aware of *one* thing, Jack Haldane," said Jane Castle, an eyebrow arched knowingly. "This is not a *date* date."

Jack Haldane slouched against her doorframe, thumbs in his pockets, grinning. "You don't like the flowers, then?"

"The flowers are lovely," said Jane, pert nose sniffing above the bouquet of exotic alien flowers. They'd cost Jack a mint, and they were worth it. Danaein mirror petals and xarnax breath and Demeter daisies subtly blended a complex spectrum's worth of color into a Escherean rainbow. The fragrances had been blended into a perfume calculated to resemble human pheromones and thus trigger amorous response. "And you, sir, are a dashingly handsome young man. There would seem to be absolutely no reason in the universe, I, a young female of the *homo sapiens* species persuasion should not immediately drag you into my boudoir, declare my eternal devotions, and perform a dance akin to the Aldebaran Mating Gymnasts at third Satellite-Rise, with the active participation of your manly attributes." She took a whiff of the flowers.

Oh speed on, flavoids! thought Jack. *Spread your gentle wings and tickle this young girl's fancy.*

He'd promised himself to remain impassive, cool this whole evening, a statue of virtue, a mere chaperone to an evening of cultural enlightenment.

Now, alas, with Jane Castle standing out of her usual asexual uniform, and in a lovely dress, her hair lifted from its usual confines and combed into a beautiful waterfall of highlighted reddish brown. Now with Jane Castle looking like an angel built for male delight alone, he couldn't help but fall right back into howling wolf mode.

Oh well . . .

You can't deny your genes or your chemistry!

"There's just two little problems that we're both quite aware of."

The police officer, in black-tie evening dress now instead of blues and spit-polishes, boosted himself from the doorjamb of Jane Castle's apartment.

"Refresh my memory," said Jack Haldane.

"One, we work together. We must display nothing but a professional attitude at all times for the benefit of our important positions as representatives of Earth people, posted here on the Demeter City Police Force."

"Detail. Number two?"

"As I've told you innumerable times, Mr. Haldane, you're simply not my type!"

"Jack. Please. Rejection is so much friendlier when it's done on a first-name basis."

"Oh, Jack. Rejection . . ." She looked sheepish and sniffed at her bouquet. "Isn't that . . . that . . . too *mild* a term?"

He laughed.

Pulled out an envelope.

"Got the tickets right here."

She was wearing a pink chiffon something, with matching high heels and a white sash. Her shoulders were bare, as was part of her chest: not indecently, but showing just enough skin to reveal the fact that it was very nice skin indeed, not too pale, but rather a creamy, human shade resonant with youth and future, passion and promise.

They were two cops in mufti, going out on a date that was not a date. And although Jack Haldane knew what the boundaries for his hands were, his imagination and his heart were unfettered. He knew that just an evening in the casual company of this beautiful, clever, and totally incomprehensible woman was going to be—well, fun.

"Come on in," she said. "I'll just get my wrap. Might be a bit of a chill in the summer breeze tonight in Demeter City, I hear."

"Sure. Thanks."

He stepped into her apartment.

Predictably sleek and neat, with a show for design and simplicity, it was a mixture of twenty-first century Earth easy-on-the-eye lines with the surprising spots of alien imagery and color she'd picked up in her years here, riding in this synchronously orbiting "suburban" satellite above Demeter City, crossroads of the known galaxy. This oddly canted vase, resplendent with angle and shifting color. That splash of crisscrossing sculpture, just above the 3-D set. Jack knew that Jane took regular drives on her off-hours into Demeter City to bizarre markets and alien bazaars to dig up these sorts of things, and also to study the art forms of the galaxy. A little hobby of hers, she claimed. Something to relieve the monotony of desk duty under the tyranny of Captain Podly at the Space Precinct.

She went to the closet, pulled out a lovely coat wrap skein with a spiderweb-like tracery of subtle sparkles that somehow managed to be diaphanous one moment and opaque the next. It moved over her breasts like a languid lover.

Jack Haldane envied it like hell.

"So tell me again. How did I get myself inveigled into going to this intriguing event with someone I'm emphatically not interested in?"

"Simple," said Jack. "It was Took that arranged it."

"Hello, Tookie. Move over, *Hello Dolly*—well, I never thought of our Tarn private police colleague as a matchmaker . . . but it looks as though she's started out on the wrong foot—or whatever term Tarns use for ambulatory peds."

Jack had never seen one without shoes.

Jack also had never seen Tarns out of their clothes. Alas, he'd seen some Creons, though, from picture books Orrinn would ogle from time to time at coffee breaks. Pretty hair-raising stuff. Of course, when Jane bent over to get at a file cabinet, alien heads wouldn't turn either—only Jack's and the occasional human's—including Patrick Brogan's. (Though of course Haldane would never mention that to Brogan's wife, Sally.)

The Tarns and the Creons were the controlling races here on Demeter City. Neither race originated on the planet Altor, where Demeter sprouted like overgrown permacrete and glassteel fungus across a large part of a continent. Altor, however, was at a key point in the galactic byways and the fortunate Tarns and Creons had built Demeter as a refuge from their far less rich home planets, Simter and Danae.

Demeter City had quickly become a trading crossroads, and more alien races had emigrated here, but by far Tarns and Creons were in the majority. Unfortunately, the money accumulating had brought criminals as well. Along with the usual urban problems, law enforcement was a problem here. That was one of the reasons humans were brought to Demeter. Earth people might have a sorry history of wars and holocausts and general misery—however, mankind had somehow developed police forces and methods of criminology unsurpassed in the galaxy.

It was only natural that there should be an exchange program instituted.

Jane Castle had come over with the first wave. Jane was from London. London police were seen as the most civilized of police forces. Indeed, many of their systems worked tremendously well with Demeter's problems. Alas, Demeter was far more like another famous Earth city, and radical measures were taken.

Demeter City imported New York City cops.

Jack Haldane and Patrick Brogan were New York cops. Good ones.

They were making a difference now on Demeter. A *big* difference. They were introducing all kinds of interesting Big Apple traditions into the tough streets of Demeter, and by and large they were impressing the Demeter City Police Force . . . yet, alas, not Jane Castle, who occasionally found them a little heavy-handed.

New York City cops on an alien planet.

Hey. What could be more natural?

Sometimes, back in his early days, he'd thought New York City was an alien planet!

"Well, I must say, it's a fortunate fact that this performance is something, A: I've never seen before; B: I've always heard about, but thought only Tarns could attend."

"Apparently, it's a great honor not to be a Tarn and still get a seat . . . to say nothing of a seat so close to the stage," said Jack.

"There will be honored guests of various species at this special performance of the Tarn Ceremonial Performance of their Inter-Mind Dance/Song SOUL/HEART—and we're to be included . . . thanks no small amount of persuasion on my part with our dear bud Took."

"Yes. Right. That's the way—take sole credit."

"Hey! You've been here longer than I have, and how many times have *you* been invited to the SOUL/HEART? Hmm?"

"I'm sure it was just an oversight."

"Maybe before they just didn't think you had a soul . . . much less a heart. Maybe, when I strode in, Took could not help but telepathically notice the flutter-flup of those relatively cholesterol-clear valves."

"In your dreams!"

"You know, Castle—they say that the SOUL/HEART is the most romantic piece of performance art ever to be conceived in the minds of sentient beings."

"Well, take my word for it, chum. This piece of performance art is *all* that's *ever* going to be conceived while we're remotely adjacent!"

Nonetheless, those gorgeous greens sparkled!

That cute nose twitched!

She was playful and alive as a young fawn, and she *loved* this!

How long would it take before her true feelings would peel back like delicate petals . . . ?

Hmm. A long time, probably.

He'd settle tonight, actually, for a good-night kiss.

But then, the sweet smell of her naturally made his hormones and fantasies yearn for much more.

"Now, now! Peace! Peace! That's all I ask for! Let a little more of that fondness you've admitted shine forth this evening. Lest this sacred performance be sullied . . . like yon bottom burp in a baptismal pool!"

"Shakespeare, watch out. A new bard is born—Ooops, sorry. I meant *bored.* " She laughed. "Well, we'd better be going or Took will be wondering if we're doing something disgusting together."

"Oh, anything we might do together, by its very nature, would be wonderful, fulfilling, and totally natural. In sync with the ebb and flow of the Universe, the yin and yang of existence." He waggled an eyebrow at her. "In short, fantastic."

"Oooh . . . Really?" She gave a pause for reflection. "Fantastic, you say? You know, I like a man who has a grasp of philosophy, of what's important in life."

Haldane bobbed his head, jabbed his chest with his thumb. "That's me!"

"And you said you'd do *anything* with me?" She touched his arm, smoothing the material, clearly relishing the strong firm biceps therein. "*Anything* I want, and it would be fulfilling for you?"

Images flooded Jack Haldane's love-starved mind. His pulse quickened. Philosophy! He'd always known that Castle had an Achilles heel somewhere—but he didn't realize it would be in the land of Plato and Aristotle and Lao-tzu.

"Sure! I'm nimble not merely in mind."

"And *very* athletic, I'm sure!"

"I've had no complaints."

She took a finger and toyed with his strong chin, dragged it down his neck, played with his tie. "You may just be the physical specimen of my fantasies. Perhaps after the show, we might grab a bottle of bubbly . . . cozy up here with a few interesting devices I acquired recently . . . ?"

Haldane thought he might very well faint from overexcitement.

"Sure! Anything . . . I promise . . . You won't be sorry . . . Say we've got a couple of spare minutes . . . Why don't you give me a sample?"

"Can you stand my love games, Jack?"

"Jane, it's hard to live without them."

She stepped back, beckoning. "That's a promise?"

"Sure. Of course."

Maybe it was the flowers that did the trick. Flowers and philosophy! A deadly combo!

She led him back into her bedroom. He was vaguely aware of pink and frilly things, stuffed animals, juxtaposed oddly with alien art pieces. However, he was mostly focused on her smile, her charms.

In front of her bed was a table.

On the table was a box.

"I never thought you'd be man enough to handle these, Jack, but since you've promised to try. When we get back, you'll know my deepest secret."

Jane Castle turned back the lid of the box.

Tiles.

Black tiles with white dots.

"Dominoes?" said Jack Haldane, astonishment throwing a bucket of cold water upon passion.

"Oh, yes, Jack. We'll have a hot evening!"

He gritted his teeth, realizing he'd been had. "Not even strip dominoes, I suppose."

"Oh, I really have no desire to see you lose your shirt, Jack."

He turned on his heel, stalked from the room.

"Okay, okay. Dominoes and champagne after the show. A promise is a promise."

He couldn't believe she'd had him on like that!

Once again, the Haldane curse: testosterone triumphant!

Intellect abandoned.

She'd never do this again, he swore.

Never.

"There's a good lad, Jack," she said, hurrying along after him, closing the door, and passing the magnilock over it. They walked along to the turbolift in heavy silence for a moment, a dark cloud riding above Haldane.

"Uhmm . . . Jack?" she said meekly, perhaps even penitently.

"Yeah . . . What?" His gruffness relented slightly.

"You *do* know how to play dominoes, don't you?"

He gave a glib smirk. "Why don't we just wait and see about that, Officer Castle? In the meantime, perhaps we might discuss a little wager on the matter?"

"Oh, but my daddy always taught me: The Wagers of Sin is Death."

"You're in the Valley of the Shadow already, Officer Castle," said Haldane, a smile bringing his cocksureness back to full brightness. "Now why don't you move that beautiful dress and that mischievous little mind into the turbolift? There's a little matter of a performance of the Tarn persuasion we have to deal with."

"Sure, Officer Haldane. Oh, lord, how I love a dominoed male."

She giggled.

Haldane steamed.

CHAPTER 5

The sound hung in and around the hall like layers of a delightful curtain.

Jack Haldane had noticed it the moment he'd stepped out of the parking structure within sight of the Tarn Arts and Municipal PanStellar Hall. It was like a melody without a tune, a mood without a body, a soul that quietly and gently wrapped itself around you and said, "Relax."

"Psi generator," said Jane Castle matter-of-factly, finally breaking the silence she'd maintained since the hopper ride.

"Pardon?" said Haldane. He was a bit overwhelmed. Tarn Arts Hall was a magnificent cathedral of geometric forms and colors, with flying buttresses and cupolas and altogether more than the eye could take in and concentrate on singly. Together, though, the effect of all the stimuli was amazing and beautiful, subtly accessible yet indefinably alien.

"I know you can feel it—the kind of, well, music in the air, the good feeling. Took told me about it. She was wondering if it would have any effect on humans in this kind of environment. It certainly has an effect on me, and I can tell it has an effect on you."

"I'm just gawking at the architecture and the art." They had shown their tickets to elaborately garbed guards and were now walking along with the nicely dressed crowd through a carpeted garden of statues. Crystalline statues gleaming with spectra, bronze masterpieces of Tarn abstracts, clay busts—a panoply of stunning achievement. That this was obvious even to Jack Haldane, who had napped all the way through Art Appreciation in college, made it all the more impressive.

"No. Seriously. I can *sense* it. I can tell it touches you as well."

"Something sure is making me feel—different. And it is sorta like music." Jack grinned. "Say! Jane! Are you saying that you admit we're on the same wavelength?"

"I'm saying nothing of the sort. Maybe it's because we're both just human, Jack. Is that okay with you? To be just human. To share things together . . . merely in our humanity. I mean, as long as we're together tonight, we might as well."

She smiled at him. Linked her arm in his.

Her touch was magic. He was astonished at the way it affected him. He fell quiet as he escorted her through the art garden into the foyer of the hall. Here were many individuals, dressed in jewels and finery, milling and chatting. Most were Tarn, but there were a few Creons here and there, and a few other peoples.

However, as far as Haldane could tell, he and Castle were the only humans present. Working in a largely alien city had always been nothing less than strange—but then, that was part of his job. Socializing with all aliens was something he wasn't quite used to. Having Castle along now wasn't just for amorous purposes: he felt a real comfort in her humanity.

"You want a drink before we go in?" said Haldane, gesturing toward what amounted to a fancy concession stand. Haldane liked concession stands, alien or not. He wondered if they had hot dogs with ketchup.

"I'm fine, thanks," said Castle. "My, what a gathering. There's a feeling of anticipation, of greatness in the air, isn't there, Jack?"

Jack! She'd called him Jack! His heart fluttered. "Uhm, yeah, boy, there sure is, Jane."

She seemed totally absorbed in it all, mesmerized. "I've always been interested in the Tarn culture, Jack. Ever since I've been here. They're not quite open, you know? They're warm, true, and perceptive—but aloof." She rubbed his back, smiled at him. "Thanks for getting me in here. Took must have owed you a favor, eh?"

"Uhm—yeah. Right."

Actually, truth was, little Tookie was a matchmaker and that was just A-OK with Jack Haldane if it got him a date with Jane Castle . . . even if it really wasn't a date.

"Say—there she is!" said Castle.

Jack scanned, saw the demure, pretty Tarn talking to some other Tarns by a huge portrait of some kind of Tarn royal family.

"You bet!" he said. He started waving. "Hey! Tookie! We're here."

As neighboring aliens stared disapprovingly, Castle cringed and grabbed his arm. "Haldane. The Tarns have a sense of protocol and decorum. You can't just act like you're at Dodger Stadium here."

"Oh. Yeah. Sorry."

"That's all right. I just hope they don't get the wrong impression of humans. You'll promise to be on your best behavior, won't you?"

"Sure. I won't do my Bronx cheers or anything, Jane. Honest."

She looked relieved. "Just refrain from your normal New York enthusiasms, Haldane. That will be quite sufficient. Now, let's go over and say hi to Took!"

They made their way through a crowd. There was a butlerlike guy carrying a tray of glasses and goodies in one hand. Haldane thought about grabbing himself something, but stopped as soon as Castle shot him a warning look.

He stuck his hands in his pockets.

"Took," said Castle. "Sorry to disturb you. But we're here!"

"Hi, Took," said Haldane.

The Tarn police officer was, of course, out of uniform now, and she looked magnificent in a flowing chiffon dress. She smiled radiantly and her blue eyes twinkled with warm delight.

"Jane! Jack! I'm so glad you could come."

She quickly introduced her guests to a couple of Tarn males, who looked stoic and monklike, barely saying a thing but hello. Haldane lifted his hand from his pocket to shake hands, but then halted himself. Did Tarns shake hands? Who knew? Better not to try.

Took excused them from the conversation, and then guided them toward the entrance of the hall. "You've come at *exactly* the right moment. There's more than enough time to find our seats and get comfortable."

Took was a very comely example of the Tarn race, the most aesthetically pleasing bunch that Haldane had encountered so far in his galactic experiences. She had pale skin, no nose, pointy ears, and looked rather like an elf might. Her eyes were quite beautiful—all three of them. Haldane had only seen her third eye a few times. It was in the middle of her forehead and generally opened only when she was focusing her telekinetic powers. She had the most expressive smile that Haldane had ever seen.

"That's wonderful, Took," said Castle. "I'm *so* looking forward to this! I'm quite fascinated with the Tarn culture."

"It's only just getting possible to allow humans to these kinds of functions, Jane," said Took pleasantly. "We're a gentle race in general, and particularly sensitive in the upper registers of psychic abilities . . ."

"Kind of like upper classes, huh, Took? Being from England, Jane could probably relate to that."

"Not quite. It's not privilege really, or breeding—

but sensitivities. There are plenty of rough Tarns with powerful powers of the mind. But to truly enter into the realm of finesse in regard to the finer aspects of psi—well, it's complex and something I suspect you'll be learning something about tonight."

"You will explain some of the finer points, won't you?" said Castle. "Also give us some background."

"And the cast recording, too as a souvenir?"

"Haldane," said Castle sharply. "This isn't the Neil Simon Theater on Broadway. Think of it as a church."

"Hey! I've heard of churches that *make* you buy the cast recording!"

Castle glared daggers.

Took laughed. "Oh, it's a spiritual and traditional affair, this Tarn ceremony—but please . . . you needn't be *terribly* reverent. This is more of a family affair." She pointed over to a Tarn couple. In the mother's arms was a Tarn baby. It smiled and waved at Haldane.

Haldane waved back. "Cute kid. Bet it cries in the middle of the quiet part. Kids always do."

"Children are welcome because it's a part of their heritage," explained Took. "You'll see how all ages can appreciate the Ceremony of the Silent Song."

"Cool title," said Haldane. "Say—I'm kind of peckish. There wouldn't be any licorice whips or Ju Ju Bees for sale around here anywhere?"

Took looked confused.

"Confections."

Took smiled and nodded. "Oh yes. Of course. Right over here." She led them to a booth, spoke to the Tarn behind it. Credits were exchanged. A gilt-edged box was handed to Haldane.

"I hope you will find this sweet and savory enough, Jack."

Haldane opened the top, and was pleased to find a collection of colorful and glossy shapes. Unable to restrain himself, he picked out a purple one and popped it into his mouth. Flavor exploded. "Hey—kind of like chocolate coconut caramel jelly beans!" He offered the box to Castle. "Want some?"

Castle demurred.

"How about you, Took?"

"Later on, certainly," said Took. "They're my personal favorites. Right now, we'd better find our seats. This way."

She took them through a curtained doorway into an awesome auditorium. The seats and the balconies were streamlined geometrically in a way that was both alien and pleasing to the eye. The ceiling was a chiaroscuro of stripes and odd paintings, crystalline structures, colored gems—and what seemed to be lattices of mirrors. There was a pleasant odor of freshly cleaned carpet, and a large hush of something big and important about to take place here.

Took showed their tickets to a Tarn usher in a long, flowing robe, who guided them down an aisle silently and sedately.

"Kind of like a rock 'n' roll monk," said Haldane, pointing at the usher, whom he found to be a curious combo of the serene and the outrageous.

"How true," said Castle, actually nodding at his witticism.

This atmosphere seemed actually to have a calming effect on her. She wasn't all bristly and tart. Haldane rather liked it—but then, he did rather enjoy her witty barbs sometimes. Maybe he was kind of a masochist.

Maybe he just liked Jane Castle any way she cared to package her ample charms.

They went down and down carpeted steps through the steep descent, stopping finally at a row just in front of a large proscenium.

"Wow!" said Haldane. "Front row seats."

"This is just wonderful, Took!" said Castle. She looked as though she wanted to lean over and kiss her friend on the cheek, but restrained herself.

Took, though, undoubtedly able to read her emotion fairly easily, beamed with pleasure. "Thank you. I think you are in for a most elucidating experience."

The robed usher flashed a light on three seats to one side of the row. They were strangely skewed seats, but they were padded and looked comfortable enough, Haldane supposed. He waited for the two women to seat themselves, then plopped down into the seat, eager to dig into his box of goodies.

The usher handed them programs and then departed.

Haldane unscrolled the thing and stared down at the vellumlike paper. Odd symbols stared back.

"Hope you'll translate this, Tookie. Can't make heads or tails of it."

"Perhaps a little more background, too, if you don't mind," said Castle. "That would certainly enrich our experience of the concert. I want you to know how much we appreciate this, Took," she said sincerely. "I know it was probably very hard for you to convince your Elders to allow Earthfolk to attend this. I hope we'll not only be able to help our people understand yours—but that we'll also be able to represent our people properly to yours." The last had a barb in its phrasing and a perfect eyebrow arched in Haldane's direction.

He shrugged it off, leaned back in his seat, and opened his box of goodies. "Sure you don't want one?" he said.

"Later, thank you," said Castle, and Haldane popped another one in his mouth. Hmm! Kinda crunchy licorice taffy! Chewy! This one would *last!*

"Save some for me!" said Took. "Why yes, Jane, of course. I'll be glad to give you some background. I don't know how much you know. . . ."

"We'll just go to the Jack Haldane default . . . namely, not a 'whole heck of a lot,'" said Jane.

"Very well," said Took, leaning forward in her seat thoughtfully. "As you know, we Tarns have a large array of psi powers—which is to say, powers of the mind. Telepathy, psychokinesis, and of course telekinesis . . . the last of which, alas, we like to show off most. There are other darker and lighter powers of the mind beyond our brains that are vestigial at this time. Our psychic researchers experiment with these in our special mind-labs. We wish to develop peaceful sources of energy, enrich our souls . . . And perhaps even find better recipes for confections! The array of research is wide.

"Our mind powers were not always so developed. Back on our home planet, at the beginning of our civilization, tribes would join together in festivities of peace. This was after a long spell of warfare among the tribes, and it was only when it was understood that, at heart, the differences between peoples were only cosmetic and at heart, we were all one. Differences and creativity were celebrated at these festivities. Concerts were held . . . Secrets of music and mind over matter manipulation were welded together in a manner that had not only practicality but artistic qualities. The tradition continues to this day, and we hold special concerts like this one not so much to develop anything—we are a unified people now, by and large, and as I said our researches are more scientific, and we have artists to create our art—but to celebrate the evolution and the achievement and aesthetics of our people. It rather reminds us of where we've been—and helps to point us to where we are going!"

Haldane was listening to this speech intently, getting very wrapped up in it. In truth, the main reason he'd wanted to go to this concert was because he knew that Jane wanted to go, and it could be an opportunity to be with her in a social setting. However, he had to admit, the Tarns were pretty fascinating creatures. He was getting more and more excited about the idea of finding out more of what their music was, their thoughts and dreams. After all, they made damned good candy!

Haldane was wondering what their hot dogs were like when he noticed the odd sounds coming from behind him.

Something cackling.

Something like . . . "Snorgle goo."

Mewling sounds.

"Yanx," said a woman's voice. "Now you have to remember, you have to be very, very good this evening. Do this, and your mother and father will be very *very* proud of you."

"Blatt! BLATT!" said a small but assertive voice.

Oh, no.

Haldane hesitatingly craned around to have a look around at the people sitting behind him. Indeed, it was the couple he'd seen before with the baby. The Tarn couple, the Tarn baby. Oh, rats! He *hated* when kids sat behind, in front of, or beside him when he was trying to enjoy something! Kids were okay, but they made the worst ruckus at the most inopportune times!

Even as he looked at the Tarn kid, the blue eyes of the Tarn kid looked back—

And focused.

A smile of pure delight filled the little Tarn face with sunshine. A little finger pointed at Haldane. This Yanx kid was acting like he'd either just seen the most wonderful thing he'd ever seen in his short life—

Or the absolutely perfect chump.

A little squeal of delight pealed from the cute little tyke.

A shiver of dread filled Haldane.

Quickly, he turned back and grabbed another piece of candy.

"Oh my," he could hear the woman mutter. "Did you see . . . A human . . ."

"Whew! Yes!" said the man. "Faces like fright shows!"

Haldane steamed. When you grew up good-looking, it was tough to take beings who thought you were ugly. Bit of a blow to the ego!

He tried to concentrate on what Took and Castle were talking about.

"Yes, good point, Jane," Took was saying. "It's kind of like a pageant—but, of course, there's a great deal more going on. There's the linear entertainment, of course, but there are also metaphorical and symbolic levels interweaving with multi-dimensional sensory cues in an overlay that constitutes a mathematical puzzle that in turn keys into the Book of Anagrams and presents a lovely and new Brain-poem for the true artistic and literary connoisseurs in the assemblage."

"Euuuuuu—BLATT!" cried out Yanx, the Tarn baby, in a seemingly adamant refutation of this statement.

"I agree absolutely!" said Haldane. "Send out the clowns. Blow up the balloons. Crank up the band! Any rock and roll tonight, Tookie?"

Castle glared at him. "Hal*dane*!"

Took laughed. "Don't worry, Jane. Jack's high spirits are more than welcome in the festivities. They contribute to the collective spirit of the moment. . . . I think the term that your Earth psychologists might use would be *gestalt*. Although of course it's a much stronger phenomenon with us because of our stronger mind abilities."

"Yes. And some humans have remarkably smaller mental powers than others," said Castle, looking at Haldane disapprovingly.

"I don't suppose there's some kind of program that I can use to follow along with?" said Haldane. "Maybe some kind of writing device I can doodle with?"

"I don't see any crayons or coloring books, Haldane," said Castle. "Perhaps you should ask the baby."

As though sensing that it was being talked about, the Tarn baby stuck his hand out, touching Haldane's shoulder. All three of them turned around. He smiled and burbled and giggled at them.

Castle waved. "Hi, there, little guy." She grinned at the parents. "He's very cute."

"Thank you," said mother.

"We're very sorry if he's bothering you," said the father, a slender and mild-faced fellow. "He usually settles down when the music begins."

"Yanx just *loves* music," said the mother. "That's why we bring him to concerts."

The baby's eyes seemed to fix on Haldane. It leaned forward and joyfully grabbed a hunk of Haldane's neatly coiffed hair.

"Owwwww!" said Haldane.

"Ga ga BLATTTTT!" said the baby excitedly. "Ga ga BLATT BLATTTTT!"

"Yanx!" said the mother. She managed to pull

the baby's hand away from Haldane's hair and pull the kid back.

Yanx laughed and pointed at Haldane, eyes filled with delight, as though he thought the young cop was the funniest thing he'd ever seen in his short life.

Jack Haldane was having profound W. C. Fields kinds of thoughts about children.

"Good grief," said Haldane, smoothing his hair back into place. "A hairstyling critic!"

"And a good one!" quipped Castle.

"Oh, thanks!" said Haldane.

"High spirits, just like yours, Jack," said Took. "Perhaps he's picking up your zest for life, your love for excitement, your intense anticipation to kiss Jane . . ." Took colored. "Whooops."

"Oh my. A little telepathic leak," said Castle. "Well, if he doesn't behave tonight, I'll certainly *tell* him where he can kiss me."

"Jane Castle!" said Haldane. "Please! We're in the presence of children!"

As though to affirm this, Yanx let off a delighted squeal of anticipation.

Suddenly, there was a sweep of strings.

Haldane looked up in time to see the curtain on the stage slowly de-opaquing in spots, revealing friezes of color jumbles that would move around like languid fireflies.

Then the curtain opened, revealing a stage consisting of a number of levels, each holding different sorts of backdrops and props. Specific details of any one level were vague since they were all in dim light. But then the mid-level suddenly came alight, showing plants of various exotic natures and the shimmer of a *faux*-lake with a yellow moon just lifting off the waters.

Figures descended from the ceiling.

Tarns, floating down under the control of their own mind powers. Upon telekinetic wings they lowered, gently, till they reached the floor. Immediately an intricate dance was performed. Music of a surprisingly intense yet subtle variety issued forth, seemingly from every possible direction.

Even, it seemed to Haldane, from inside his own head.

It was an awesome, though profoundly peculiar experience. Although there could be no question that this was *alien*, something in him had a peculiar affinity for it.

When he thought to look at her, he noticed that Jane Castle was immersed in the program. She leaned forward, eyes fixed on the proceedings, her pretty mouth half-open with amazement.

It made Haldane think of her differently, the way she looked now . . . She wasn't just pretty; there was a beauty and spirit here, a delightful *somethingness* that he'd never really encountered before.

Gradually, light began to flow from the sides of the stage, revealing Tarns in various curious outfits, wielding various alien instruments that looked to Haldane like enlarged pasta shapes from mutated Italians. Whatever they were, they certainly carried music that swirled and eddied with great emotional power. Trouble was, some of them were emotions that weren't particularly human and made for odd resonances in him.

After a while, he realized he was hungry.

A few of those candies would certainly do the trick.

He looked down at the box and was startled to see that it was open.

By the vague and ambient chair-light to his left and right, he saw an object floating up from his lap.

A piece of the Tarn confection!

Before his amazed eyes it floated up as though attached to some invisible marionette string. He watched as it levitated up to his eye level, then scooted over his row of chairs to the row behind.

He craned his neck, and squinted into the dimness.

Yanx, the Tarn kid behind him, happily grabbed the piece of candy in his chubby fist and crammed it into his maw. Candy juice dribbled down his chin onto the front of his shirt.

He looked like a being in total heaven.

Haldane looked down at his open box.

There was exactly *one* piece of candy left.

Hastily he reached down for it.

It jumped out of his reach, lifted into the air.

Haldane made a grab for it.

The candy dodged.

Growling, Haldane tried again.

The candy jerked away, and then, as though to taunt him, banged into his forehead. It smacked, bounced off, and then zipped back into the waiting hand of the Tarn kid.

"Hey!" said Haldane.

He reached back to grab the candy from the kid, but with a quickness that belied his extreme youth, the baby crammed it into his mouth.

Haldane yowled with frustration.

"Stay away from my baby!" cried the frightened Tarn mother.

"Haldane? *Whatever* do you think you're *doing*?" said Jane Castle.

"That blasted brat swiped all my candy," said Haldane, incensed.

Yanx stuck out his gooey tongue.

Something black went off in Haldane's mind.

However, he managed to restrain himself. He could get in real trouble here. He simply looked at the Tarn parents and said, "You really ought to watch that kid! He's a menace."

"You're the menace, Haldane," said Castle. "To interstellar relations!"

Quickly and expertly, Took smoothed ruffled feathers all around. "There's an intermission in a while," she said to Haldane. "I'll buy you a new box, okay?"

"Oh, that's all right, Tookie. I'll get one. I just got pissed that the kid was getting away with it."

He looked behind him, and there was the kid, looking pleased with himself—and looking for all the world as though he would just *love* to moon him.

Grumpily, Haldane settled back into his chair and tried to enjoy the performance.

All he could think of, though, was Tarn baby spankings.

Eventually, the splendid performance surrounding him soothed and mollified him, and he found himself swept up into its artistic embrace.

The lighting had changed, and now the Tarn singers were acting out some kind of dance-drama. There was much swooping and yodeling and groups of folks waving from one side of the stage to the other in a yin-yang parade of black and white, white and black. Haldane recognized snatches of meaning in the explosions of the Tarn language, but for the most part it all went right over his head as regards content. He just pretended it was the Tarn equivalent of a Western, sat back, and enjoyed.

So, when the monster entered, he thought it was all part of the show.

CHAPTER 6

"You know, there are certain Earth customs that I'm happy that we can do together as a family, to preserve our heritage," said Patrick Brogan. It was Saturday night, and they'd just had a wonderful family dinner of Sally's spaghetti and meatballs with an out-of-sight grated Parmesan cheese (of particular note since he himself had not only programmed it from a food constitutor, but grated it by hand). A little vino had put him into an even more convivial mood, which had brought the suggestion that had brought this activity about. "One of my favorites is this one. I remember when I used to play it with *my* dad!"

He tossed the dice.

Moved his marker.

Uh-oh.

Park Place!

Three houses.

"That'll be four hundred dollars, Dad!" said Liz, his precocious eleven-year-old daughter, holding her hand out, greed shining in her eyes.

"Isn't capitalism *keen*," said Matt, stifling a yawn as he sat in front of his own set of properties and hefty pile of Monopoly money. "Glad we're importing our own particular brand from the good ol' US of A."

Brogan counted out four bills, handed them over to Liz, whose eyes glittered with keen appreciation of victory and moolah.

"Pretty soon, Dad, I'm gonna have a hotel here . . . and then you're really gonna have to pay!" she announced regally, like some new Queen of Mean.

"Liz, really," said Sally, sweetly. "It's just a game."

"No, it's a tradition, a heritage," said Matt sarcastically.

"He sure gets cranky when he doesn't have a date, doesn't he?" said Liz. "Of course, that makes him perpetually peevish, doesn't it?"

"You just wait till you land on one of *MY* squares," announced Matt indignantly. "You'll pay then!"

"Kids, kids, really," said Brogan. "A little joshing in the spirit of fun is all very well, but let's not go for each other's jugulars, okay?"

"Just trying to keep up the spirit of the pre-Depression robber barons whose memory this game preserves," said Matt. "I mean, if there's nothing better to do on a Saturday night—sheesh, that's really *not* a Saturday night at all—we might as well remember our Earth history."

"Glad you've got your mother's academic interests," said Brogan. "But we're just not on Earth any more, Matt, and we're certainly smack dab in *all kinds* of capitalism."

"Yeah, Matt," said Liz. "When in Rome and you've got to blow, go to the vomitorium, man!"

"Liz, I don't think that's quite the phrase," said Sally.

Poor Matt. It wasn't really so much that he was homesick. He was sucking up all kinds of new knowledge and new experiences here, and was just doing very well, considering that he was many light years away from the environment he'd grown up in. They still intended to send Matt to a good university on Earth—he was an *incredibly* bright kid, and already a computer whiz—so it wasn't like he didn't know that he wasn't *stuck* here, riding in a synchronous orbit above Demeter City in this space suburb, forever and ever.

No, Matt Brogan's problem was simple.

Matt was a teenager.

And that, Brogan knew, was a problem that could only be cured by the passage of time.

Since he'd transferred himself and his family from New York City into intergalactic space to bring his cop calling to the Universe, they'd had their share of adventures and they'd learned their share about absolutely astonishing things. However, one mystery, one challenge remained to them that all humans encountered, wherever they were.

How do you remain a healthy family?

How do you keep the "dys" away from the "functional"?

With his workload it was difficult. Sally's job didn't help. However, the one blessing was that, since there were limited numbers of humans on Demeter so far (though the number was escalating), and since humans by nature enjoyed the company of their own kind, this helped cement their bonds.

Still, like all families, thought Brogan, they definitely had their problems.

While both kids were extremely smart, both were also extremely competitive. The difference in their ages and their sexes did not eliminate the antipathy. In a pinch, they'd stick up for one another, and ultimately there was a lot of love as well. However, in the picayune matters of everyday life, the sad truth was that Matt and Liz were often at each other's throats.

Their place *was* beautiful here in their space suburb. They had neighbors who were from Earth as well as even more friendly alien neighbors. They had all the modern conveniences. However, fascinating as it might be, it wasn't Earth and it wasn't home. Brogan was still a cop and that job was, if anything, even *more* dangerous and unpredictable here under the present circumstances. While they'd realized this was going to be the case before they made the decision to come here, that didn't lessen the stress that the situation now put upon their marriage.

All in all, the fact that it was working at all was

thanks to Sally. Although Brogan tried his best and worked hard to keep traditions—like the occasional game nights like this—in order to keep them together as a family, somehow Sally alone had the magic to keep things truly working.

He looked at her now, sitting like a happy queen above her pile of Monopoly holdings.

He certainly loved her a lot.

Brogan honestly doubted he'd be able to make it in the wild streets of Demeter City if he didn't know that he had Sally and the kids to come home to.

Which made him think about his partner.

"I wonder how Jack and Jane are doing tonight," he said as the play continued and Liz and Matt squabbled over some minor point.

"I don't know about those two," said Sally. "I mean, it's not really a date. You said so yourself. . . ."

Brogan shrugged. "Who knows?" He smiled slyly. "It might *become* a date, okay?"

"I'm sure that Jack would like it to. It seems to me that it's Jane that's opposed to that option."

"I for one sense a lot of electricity between those two," said Brogan.

"Well, it certainly is shocking when they get along, that's for sure," said Sally. It was her turn and she threw the dice, moved her marker.

Brogan passed GO and landed on one of his own properties. He breathed a sigh of relief.

"You know, I hate to be modern," said Sally, "but you'd think that in the twenty-first century they could update the board and the concept a bit."

"Ah, Mom," said Matt. "What do you want? Do

not pass GO at light speed? Alpha Centauri Avenue? Atomic Utilities? This is a *classic*!"

Brogan beamed with pride at his son. Matt was becoming a bit of an antiquarian, and Brogan supported that tendency all the way.

"Right. If it works, why not use it—plus you've got all the ritual associations—the tradition, you know. Heck, hon. You've got to have *some* continuity."

"Well all I can say is that if we kept all our traditions, guys, we'd still be stuck on Earth," said Sally. "There's this guy coming over to speak to the Earth among the Stars group tomorrow afternoon. Some kind of representative of a political group on Earth who objects to the rapidity with which mankind is disseminating into the stars. Sounds like he's my conservative hubby and son's cup of tea."

"I'd really like to go," said Brogan. "Have to go over some computer printouts on an important case, though. Work I brought home. And it's not like I'm not a *progressive*, dear. Just because I like old ways doesn't mean I'm not open to new ones."

"Okay. Then I'll make you fried eggs for breakfast tomorrow instead of scrambled. With sausage instead of bacon!" said Sally.

"Whoa! Let's not get into *deep* political thought here," said Brogan, who liked the same breakfast pretty much every morning. "I mean, I thought we decided that we wouldn't have those sorts of arguments."

It *was* the truth that Brogan had more of a Republican soul than a Democrat's—and vice versa for Sally. The funny thing was that although he was the more conservative (and that seemed natural, since he faced crime in the streets every day) he was the more liberal in attitude toward different beliefs than Sally. When Sally thought something was right, then it was *totally* right, no ifs, ands, or buts. She was a black-and-white kind of person as far as her convictions went, and he admired her for it.

Alas, in his life he saw all too often how things could come in various shades of gray.

However, what Patrick Brogan knew was his duty. . . .

And his duty was to keep the peace, uphold the law, and generally make things livable for decent, law-abiding souls like himself. . . .

This seemed to be an issue throughout the Universe, and most emphatically so on Demeter City, which, because of the modes of galactic transportation, had become a crossroads.

All kinds of alien peoples stopped off in Demeter.

All kinds of crime.

That's why cops were needed.

New York's Finest had become the Galaxy's Finest.

And Demeter City was the focal point of the new struggle against crime and lawlessness.

Unfortunately, he wasn't quite sure where this new business with these killings fit in. Was this just some mad serial killer on the loose?

Or was there a more pernicious background, as the business with the cult might prove?

Well, that was something they would have to discover next week.

Right now, he deserved to treat himself to time with his family.

"That's great, dear," he said, getting ready to roll again. The dice had come around to him very quickly. "Tell me what you find out . . . and we'll talk about it then."

"Of course," said Sally. "We talk about everything. That's what keeps us a family."

Brogan threw the dice, moved his marker, picked up a card.

GO TO JAIL. DO NOT PASS GO.

"Uhm," he said, showing his family the card. "Can we, uh, talk about *this*?"

They all laughed at him.

CHAPTER 7

It started as a cloud . . .

. . . and became much more.

Jack Haldane was scrunched in his chair, trying to keep track of what the heck was going on. He was enjoying the performance, kind of. It had all gotten very intense, and there was a lot of smoke sailing about in swirls. Dry ice mostly, from the quality of it—gray and misty.

So when the cloud entered tenebrously, Stage Up, he barely noticed.

No, mostly now Jack Haldane was concentrating on making amends to Jane Castle, making certain that she knew he was appreciating the finer qualities of this wonderful alien display.

"Amazing!" he would say. Then he would shift forward, stare at the stage awhile, nod as though he had just gotten something absolutely profound out of the performance. "Just majestic!"

Finally, after a few more "Wonderfuls" and "Terrifics" and "Wows," Jane turned to him, finger on her lips.

"Shhhh!" she said.

"Hey. I can't help it. I'm overwhelmed. I'm just so glad that I got to witness this! I have an entirely new appreciation for the Tarn culture! I can't wait to have a long, long talk about it with you after the performance."

"Oh, Jack. By candlelight with a bottle of wine?"

"Yeah! Why not?"

"Yeah, right. Famous last words. The road to hell is paved with melted candles and empty wine bottles."

"Slippery road. You can wear your cleats!"

"Look, Jack, you're a sweetheart, but you don't mean well. Sit back, watch the show, and spare me the vocal appreciation."

Haldane sat back, feelings hurt.

All in all, things weren't going well. He was getting attitude from the back of him, attitude from the stage, and now from his side.

What he needed was less attitude and more love.

Sulking, he sank back into his comfortably cushioned seat and stared up at the ceiling, letting the sensory experiences wash over him and immersing himself in his blue funk.

It was then that he noticed the strange black cloud.

Like a mystic leak from space, it dripped down from the top of the stage. At first it seemed to blend in with the rest of the backdrop, the smoke, and the atmosphere. A little bit of black cloud: that was all. However, it got Haldane's attention when a small skein of lightninglike light shivered through it.

Hey!

Keen special effect!

No one else seemed to notice it. They seemed much too busy being immersed in the ebb and flow of the performance. However, Haldane, who was quite distractable at the time, enjoyed the chance of viewing new SF/X. He watched intently as this inkblot cloud seeped down, occasionally lighting, dusky and mysterious, in sections.

The edges became jagged.

It spread down, like a demon wing unfurling for flight.

Haldane got a little *frisson.*

And not a good one.

There was something odd about that cloud. He wondered if it was some kind of foreshadowing of dramatic events to come in the presentation. Something like that bass theme in *Jaws.*

Dum *dum* dum *dum.*

He touched Castle's elbow. "Jane. Look at that thing coming down from the top of the stage!"

"Haldane. I'm trying to focus on the subtext!"

Jack Haldane had no idea what a subtext was. Something unimportant, probably. However, it seemed vital to Jane, and he knew he wasn't exactly on her A-list at the moment, so he'd better conform to her idea of good behavior, which meant keeping his mouth shut.

"Okay. Sorry."

He watched it nonetheless as it came down. She'd notice it eventually. How could you not notice a black Rorschach splotch when it got between you and your view—as this thing *would*.

Only it didn't.

Funny thing about the splotch was that, partway down it kind of veered off, like black smoke coming out of a vent.

It flowed off toward the ceiling and then it seemed to collect and hover, as though waiting.

Haldane watched it carefully as it moiled and squatted in the air. Was that just his imagination or were there *eyes* forming in the dark mass?

Malevolent eyes!

And were they staring down at him?

He got the shivers.

He didn't like this. Not at all.

Something *bad* was going on. He could feel it in a place inside him he hadn't realized he had feelings before.

"Took!" he whispered.

"Haldane. Please!" said Castle, now extremely annoyed.

"No. This is important," Haldane said. "Tookie, look up there on the ceiling. Is that part of the show?"

Took blinked. She looked up. Didn't seem to see anything.

"The black spot."

Took focused. "Oh dear. Yes, I see. I don't know . . ."

"It not only *looks* funny," said Haldane. "It gives me the creeps. Like a spider crawling in my head."

"My goodness, Jack," said Took. "Sounds like you're picking up psychic emanations! How marvelous. I would never have scoped you out for psi potential."

"Whatever it is, I don't like it. Maybe you'd better check it out with Tarn Central, huh? There may be some kind of oil leak in the Over-schmalz or whatever."

"Yes. I'll do just that."

However, even as they were speaking, the cloud was beginning to lower over the crowd, like a scrim or a thin net.

Electrical arcs began to travel through its veins.

Someone else noticed it.

A murmur spread through the audience.

The performance seemed to sputter as members of the troupe also noticed something unusual happening.

Suddenly, Haldane got the strangest feeling he'd ever known in his life. A total conviction erupted full blown in his head:

"It's *after* something."

"What?" said Jane.

He felt a hunger, a need: not his own. It welled demandingly above them.

"It wants to feed."

Haldane didn't know where that came from. He just blurted it.

"*What* wants to feed?"

Haldane's finger shot up.

"That!"

It had become a cloud again. A cloud with jagged edges, jagged energy.

And it was descending.

Behind them, Yanx, the Tarn baby, began to cry. The high pitched call of anxiety rose above the uneasy hubbub of the crowd. Haldane wasn't sure if he noticed it because of its fingernails-on-the-blackboard quality—or simply because he'd been sensitized to everything annoying about that kid.

Whatever, for some reason, he focused on the kid.

And turned around.

Their eyes met and locked. The baby's third eye opened.

There was terror in that third eye. It clearly sensed something dangerous, something that threatened *it*.

Haldane looked up. Sure enough, the black cloud was coming down. Condensing and descending, sparkles aglitter in the nebulous mass.

Jagged edges forming together now like outstretched claws.

"What is it?" said Castle.

"I don't know." Took's third eye opened. "Whatever it is, it's certainly not part of the show . . ."

"It doesn't look friendly."

"No. It has tremendous psychic energies. . . . Efforts to push it back or nullify it by the collective Tarn force are failing. . . ."

"Is it intelligent?" asked Castle.

"I sense a primitive but somehow . . . stunted . . .

intelligence. Attempts to communicate with it are failing."

Haldane cupped his hands together. "Just get the hell out of here, huh?" When that tactic proved fruitless Haldane turned to the others. "Maybe *we'd* better get the hell out of here."

"That may be wise," said Castle. "Besides, we'd better call in for some backup. I should have brought my communicator."

"I should have brought my blaster," said Haldane. "Damn, that's one nasty—"

Without warning, a streamer of darkness sped down from the main mass. Like a tongue from a lizard, it wrapped around the Tarn baby, yanking him up away from his mother's arms.

The baby screamed as he was hoisted up.

"Oh damn," said Haldane. With no further complaint, though, he hopped up onto his seat and, with his strong legs thrusting him, leaped up toward the streamer.

The part that held the baby afforded a handhold. The black stuff of the thing buzzed and vibrated with energy, but it was solid enough now. Haldane felt himself being quickly hoisted higher and higher in the air.

The baby was squalling, but suddenly he stopped and he was staring down at Haldane with a totally sober and intent look in his little eyes.

"Hal*dane*!" cried Castle. "What *are* you doing?"

"Running for office," said Haldane. "I've *gotta* kiss this baby!"

The baby reached out and touched Haldane.

There was a sudden arc of energy. Sparks zapped.

Some kind of inhuman shriek filled the air.

The stuff that was holding them both up in the air abruptly became tenuous. Haldane felt himself slipping.

A quick look down.

He was a good twelve meters above the seats.

Haldane looked back up.

The floating creature was becoming a flimsy cloud once more, lightning shuddering through its form. It seemed to be streaming out of the hall again through some aperture . . . escaping from something it didn't care for. Like an octopus on the ocean floor, heading for some sea cave, covering its watery tracks with a blast of ink.

"Kid! Grab on!"

The kid reached out, a big grin splitting its face.

Haldane grabbed him.

"Castle!" he cried. "Catch!"

And then, holding on to the baby, Jack Haldane fell.

CHAPTER 8

The first thing Jack Haldane saw when he woke up was the face of an angel.

"Jack," she said. "Jack, how do you feel?"

He stared up blearily. "Okay, I guess." He worked his jaw and stared up blearily some more. He vaguely recognized the person's face and voice, but he couldn't be sure. Something was gumming up his eyes. He reached his hand up to wipe his eyes.

He felt dull pain in his side.

He couldn't move his arm.

His eyes shot open with alarm.

"Don't be alarmed, Officer Haldane," said a soothing, avuncular voice. "You've had an accident."

"Accident, nothing! He's a hero!"

Haldane recognized *that* voice.

Lieutenant Patrick Brogan. His partner.

Connections were made. Eyes were open wider. Haldane lifted his head, saw the people standing around him. He was on a hospital bed. Hospital accoutrements hung or sat in the predominantly white and cool-colored environment. That telltale antiseptic-and-starched-sheets smell hung in the air. Apparently certain elements of hospitals were the same throughout the galaxy.

Standing to the other side of the bed was Jane Castle, looking pretty and pretty concerned. She wasn't wearing her evening dress. Just a blouse and jeans. Brogan was in his off-duty clothes as well. Beside Brogan was a Creon doctor, looking officious and in charge. Behind him was Took and a Tarn nurse.

"Hate to be clichéd," said Haldane. "But what happened?"

"You don't remember the strange creature that attacked the Tarn Concert Hall, Jack?" said Took.

"Tookie, I've been seeing strange creatures ever since I *arrived* on this planet," said Haldane.

However, something clicked into place even as he spoke.

The rumbling, lightning-ribbed thing, descending. The cry of the baby. The strike.

Haldane stiffened. "The kid!"

"You remember!" said Castle, looking very relieved.

"As I predicted. Any amnesia would be ephemeral," said the doctor, looking pleased with himself. "This is indeed a strong specimen of your species. It was a pleasure working on him."

"Yanx!" repeated Haldane. "What happened to Yanx?"

"He's all right," said Took.

"He's been kept in the next room. No harm at all. . . . The way you held him protected him from the fall," said Jane. "You, unfortunately, took whatever force there was, banging into that row of chairs. That's how you broke your arm."

Broken arm. Of course. Haldane looked over at his arm, saw it was in a cast. A high-tech, aesthetically pleasing cast, not the old plaster-of-paris type at all—but a cast nonetheless. Otherwise, he seemed pretty much in one piece.

"I tried to break your fall with my telekinesis," said Took. "But you were coming down fast and I was only partially successful."

"Thanks, Tookie," said Haldane. "Probably saved my life. Well, glad to save the kid. But what *was* that thing?"

"That's a damned good question," said Brogan. "We've got an all-points bulletin out, looking for it—but how do you grab ahold of what's essentially an energy creature that can change into matter at will? That's the gist of what we've been able to glean from the tape playbacks."

"It's like nothing that's ever been seen on Demeter City before," said Took. "I checked this morning. In fact, it's like nothing we've seen before in the known Universe, period."

"What did it want the kid for? That's the question."

Haldane knew that. "Funny. That's what I sensed. . . . It wanted to absorb energy. And that kid—it had just the kind of psychic energy it wanted. That's why it snatched it away. It probably intended to drag him up to Beast Brain Central, suck him dry as a husk, then drop him and skedaddle."

"That's the Collective's opinion as well," said Took.

"And we also noticed something. Although our efforts against it, psychically speaking, were for naught—for some reason, you and Jane generated some kind of psychic power that it couldn't deal with. That and *only* that is why it released the baby."

Castle shook her head, clearly still trying to come to grips with this startling and perhaps upsetting notion. "Pretty hard to swallow."

Normally the idea of a psychic bond and collaboration with a beautiful woman like Jane Castle would have given Haldane, in his present girlfriendless condition, great pleasure. However, at the moment he was far too busy recollecting the actual details of the previous evening.

. . . that splotch of darkness and energy and malevolence . . .

. . . that throbbing of essence . . .

. . . that hunger . . .

. . . falling . . .

. . . a flash of pain . . .

. . . and then, darkness, nothingness, unmarred by dreams . . .

A shudder ran through him. He was very glad that he was an impetuous sort, that he'd been trained well. Faced with that awful thing now, he didn't know if he'd be able to conjure up the same kind of heroics.

Well, might as well collect all the flowers and kisses he could.

"Oh, come on Jane. We make a good team."

Took nodded soberly. "Yes, and a good thing, too . . ." She let that hang, as though considering uttering something more, but not entirely sure of how to do so.

"What *was* that thing?" said Haldane. "Any clue at all . . . ?"

"Some kind of psychic energy creature," said Brogan, thoughtfully. "We haven't got a whole lot to go on at the Force, but the Tarns are working on it."

"Ah. Like a Collective Mind Net."

"Precisely. It's clearly a beast of mind and energy. . . . And that's the area of Tarn expertise. . . ."

"Meanwhile we've got a new threat running around," said Castle. "Wonderful. A new wrinkle in crime."

"Yes. And who knows where it will strike," said Brogan.

"It's hungry and it's wild. It *will* strike again. Right now, we're just trying to determine if it's ever struck *before*." Brogan's brow was wrinkled. He had a consternated look on his face, as though he was trying to puzzle things out.

"Well, one thing I'm pretty sure about. And I've spoken to the Elders about this as well," said Took, looking solemn. "If that thing—whatever it is—was attracted by Yanx's energy, and picked him out there, in the midst of an entire hall of Tarns . . . Well, it's going to be able to pick him out somewhere else. . . . And it's going to try to snatch him again."

"Whew," said Haldane. "That could be true. I hope that the parents are well connected and can protect the poor little guy."

"*That's* a problem," said Took.

"Yes, I can see that," said Castle.

"I have the feeling important information is being withheld here," said Haldane. "So give already."

"Sadly, in its violent departure," said Took, "the creature dislodged chunks of the ceiling. We avoided injury. However, Yanx's parents, as well as others, did not."

"They weren't *killed*, were they?" said Haldane.

"No. However, both received head injuries and are presently in hospital beds in comas," said the Creon doctor. "We expect both to recover. But we have no idea when."

Took expelled a great sigh. "Which is why we have to ask you to perform a service for us—both you and Castle. A service as members of the Demeter City Police—and as fellow beings of a United Galaxy."

"Why am I getting a bad feeling about this?" said Haldane.

"We need you to help guard Yanx," said Took. "Guard him from any further attack of this creature. Jane and Jack—you apparently generate some kind of special mind field between the two of you, an energy that repels this creature. It worked last night and is honestly about the only thing that we can think that might work in the present situation."

"Oh dear," said Castle, color draining from her face.

"Guard . . . Guard that *obnoxious* baby!" said Haldane. "Protect that little *horror*!"

"You didn't seem to mind the other night!"

"I was doing my job . . . I was just . . . well, being *me*. But, I mean . . . he *stole my candy*!"

"Oh my, oh my!" said Brogan, clucking. "What a little monster!" He smiled warmly and understandingly. "On the other hand, take it from me, kids are *great*. And who knows . . . maybe this thing won't even bother Yanx or you. Besides, with that arm of yours, this is just about the only kind of duty you're going to be able to perform, Jack."

"What about *me*, though," said Jack. "I'm mean—I'm injured in the course of duty. Don't I get time off!"

"I've never had a child!" said Jane. "I've never had little sisters or brothers. I've never *dealt* with a baby before, much less a *Tarn* baby!"

Brogan shook his head. "Yes, but there it is. I don't think this is a matter of volunteer work, here, guys. You seem to be the only people for the job. . . . We've already arranged for special facilities for you to stay in. Also special nurses for both you and the baby, so you won't exactly have to worry about diaper duty."

"Wait a just one darned minute," said Jack. "All my time in the force, I've never so much as reported a stubbed toe! Now, when I've got a genuine disability period, time when I should be able to kick back, have some R and R, you want me to hang around a mischievous child?"

"Ah, nurses," said Jane. "Hmm. That's not so bad then. Well, Jack . . . I guess we're going to have to bite the bullet. We're clearly the people picked out for this task. If I can put up with you, you can put up with Yanx." She smiled. "Besides, *I* think he's adorable."

"Good," said Took. "The Grand Council will be so pleased. Your valiant efforts have already done wonders in Tarn-Terran relations. This will surely open up whole new vistas."

"I'm puzzled about one thing," said Jane. "If this creature is roaming Demeter City, to keep Yanx safe why not simply take him off planet? Like maybe to your space suburb, Lieutenant."

Haldane nodded. "Good point." He looked over to Brogan, who was now wearing a frown.

"Yes, well, that was certainly considered," said Brogan. "However, there *is* a matter which we haven't brought up yet—and I suppose we should be honest with you both about it now.

"We've examined the damage this energy thing created at the Tarn Hall. Results are inconclusive, but there may be reason to believe that *this* is the thing that's been causing the rash of deaths in Demeter City."

That little bit of news hung in the air like something heavy and ponderous and unwelcome.

"If it comes for Yanx again, we're hoping to be ready to neutralize it," Brogan finished.

Haldane blinked. "You mean, we're guarding *bait*!"

"I don't think it's necessary to look at it in quite that manner," said Took. "This matter has been brought up before the Council this morning—and in fact it was they who suggested it. A threat of this magnitude—Well, if something like this is stalking Demeter City . . . it must be stopped!"

Haldane nodded. "Yeah. I guess you're right." He shrugged. "Sorry about the doubts. . . . But when you put it that way, I'm all gung ho."

"Nothing wrong with a little fear, friend," said Brogan. "It's human and it's healthy."

"It's not so much fear of that thing that bothers me—it's that kid. . . . Without its parents . . . Unchecked . . . What's it going to be *like*?"

"That's something I suppose we're going to be finding out very soon . . . Dad!" Jane smiled.

"I can hardly wait!" said Haldane.

He looked at his cast and sighed.

CHAPTER 9

Sally Brogan found a seat at the assembly and then sipped thoughtfully at her cup of tea as she waited for the speaker to come out.

Normally she attended this kind of Sunday afternoon political address with one of her friends from her group, but for one reason or another none of them had been able to make it today. Near the concession stand she'd spoken to some of the other Earth people who'd attended. She knew many of them casually, but she was surprised at how many she hadn't known. In fact, she was surprised at the turnout here at this hotel meeting room.

There were a lot of humans here, a lot of Earth people.

And no other races.

Funny. Although she was with her own kind, she felt kind of odd now, not seeing Creons or

Tarns in a group this large on Demeter City. She was used to other races now . . . and she had stopped thinking of them as aliens . . . especially Tarns and Creons. She just thought of them as fellow, well, *beings*. There was so much that they had in common—and yet there was so much to be learned from their differences.

True, her life here on and above Demeter City was a great deal more complicated than it had been back on Earth. But then, the opportunity had been too great to pass up. They'd made a commitment to stick it out, and even though stress and upset and surprise were constant parts of the recipe, there were rewards as well.

Many rewards.

And knowledge and experience *far* beyond what she'd ever realized she'd attain in her youth, growing up in a small town on Long Island and then attending a state-run university.

The odd thing was that she'd never been very good in astronomy. Now she was far more intimate with the stars than her teachers had ever been.

"Good afternoon!" said a cherry-cheeked, heavy-set woman wearing a no-nonsense business suit. "We're so happy to see such a good turnout for assembly today. It's a challenge indeed to live such a long way from home, and our group has been quite successful so far in providing comfort and human affiliation in a land that is not our own." She sniffed, touched her nose with a lace handkerchief, then turned a warm welcoming smile back onto the audience. "However, it's always *so* nice to have a visitor from Earth to remind us who we are, where we're from—and what's going on back there.

"Joseph Salamander's is a name that is no secret to anyone from the United States of America. He served two consecutive terms as speaker of the House of Representatives. He now has his own Comm Highway show, 'The Salamander Hour,' and a stirring string of best-selling books and tapes. He is the president of the Earth Philosophy Organization, with a long list of honors. Now, he is on a fact-finding mission to experience firsthand the human role in intergalactic affairs.

"Ladies and gentlemen, I am indeed deeply honored to present before you for his first speech *off* the planet Earth . . . the Honorable Joseph Salamander. . . ."

A man stepped through a door and merrily hopped up the steps to the podium, where he gave an enthusiastic handshake to his introducer. He was a big guy, with short gray hair. His eyebrows were bushy and emphatic, riding over intense blue eyes that seemed to reach out at the whole audience and pin them to their seats with their intensity.

He took a deep breath and let it out.

"Ah . . . The smell of humanity is sweet. It's so good to be among you today. I don't remember feeling so welcome . . . I've been here for a week now, and I can sense how close this alien experience is bringing you people, knitting you into a community that is truly a wonderful representative of our dear planet.

"There are exciting things going on back on Earth, my friends. Our knowledge of the existence of other civilizations is bringing *our* governments, *our* peoples together into an appreciation of what it means to be human."

A self-satisfied grin filled his big face and he took a moment to look out upon the intent listeners.

"And we're feeling pretty damned good about being human, believe me.

"You know . . . I've been touring about for a while here . . . And I studied the tapes and books and information that had been sent me before. I have certainly seen some wondrous things here on Demeter City . . . I have most certainly met some marvelous sentient aliens who have built this city, standing here on this crossroads. Wondrous and marvelous though they be, it makes me appreciate how magnificent is the heritage and destiny of the human heart, the human mind.

"For while we have much to learn from the civilizations and cultures beyond our dear sun Sol—it is my sincerest belief that they have even more to learn from us."

He gripped the podium intently and leaned forward into the mike and spoke in a commanding baritone in the tones of a practiced and expert speaker.

"We should all feel *very* proud of what we've given to the Universe," he said. He paused dramatically, then spoke in a carefully controlled, quieter, cautious tone. "At the same time, perhaps it would be best not to give . . . too much.

"We humans, by nature, are trusting, open people. And for that reason . . . and for many, many others which I won't recount here for fear of being simply a cheerleader for our qualities of character, our diverse dimensions of intelligence . . . perhaps, in our joy and eagerness to be introduced to the wonders and byways of the galaxy, we have been a bit too naive, a bit less appreciative of what *we* have to offer the universe at large.

"For this reason, I sincerely believe that it is a time for us all to pause and reflect upon what the true situation now is—and where we, as humans upon Earth, and now humans among the stars, stand."

Sally Brogan considered herself, if nothing else, a practical woman. Although the tenet "Do unto others as you would have them do unto you" was a golden rule to some, it just seemed to Sally to be common sense. Her liberal politics worked for her simply because they *worked*. If things weren't right now, then you just did what you could—or helped create a system—that would make them right. In her view, the future was the place for *improvement*, *progress*, not backpedaling.

All this that Salamander was saying sounded suspiciously like something she'd hoped a jump to the stars would take out of human beings. The vantage point obtained from such a lofty perch, she hoped, would give mankind wisdom.

Alas, it was clear that many—including former politicians and talk show hosts—would much prefer getting back into their shells.

As she sipped her cooling but still aromatic tea, she listened to the speaker. Salamander continued along the same thread, promoting the place of mankind in the Universe, suggesting that humans "keep the human gene pool pure" and generally other cloaked racist . . . no, *speciesist* . . . statements.

"May I conclude by inviting you all to form a chapter of my new organization . . . The Measure of Man, based on that famous Protagoras quote. . . . The purpose of 'The Measure of Man' is to promote the cause of humanity, whether on Earth or among the stars. There is a register for the interested here, and you most certainly may avail yourself of my tapes and books here . . . all, of course, for a small fee. It is a truly human thing, after all, to be a capitalist."

He grinned charmingly, and there was laughter.

"We are also in great need of volunteers to continue the expansion of The Measure of Man here and, of course, anywhere else that mankind may go. Those of you who wish to sign up in the back, I will personally shake your hand and meet with you and give you my deepest thanks."

Salamander finished up with a rousing series of quotes from such luminaries as William Shakespeare, the Bible, Abraham Lincoln, and Rush Limbaugh, and then, to deafening applause, descended to the backstage receiving area to perform his promised greetings to the truly faithful.

Although they seemed to enjoy his speech, only a few of the crowd seemed inclined to volunteer.

This was gratifying to Sally, but still the poison in the air remained, however sugar-coated.

As did her curiosity.

This slimy Salamander guy was here on Demeter City for more reasons than to push his books. Her intuition told her that much. It wasn't that he was breaking the law or anything, so she couldn't exactly sic her husband on the man.

But he was up to something, and something profoundly against Sally's sense of what was correct behavior for humans in the midst of alien hospitality.

There was only one way she could hope to find out what that something was.

She went back and signed up as a volunteer.

"Well, how do you do!" she heard a voice behind her say just as she was finishing up adding her name, address, and communications number to the list. She turned around, and found herself face-to-florid-face with Joseph Salamander in the flesh.

And there was a lot of flesh, most of it now flushed and grinning and slightly perspiring.

She hadn't really expected to actually meet the Man herself, so her surprise was honest, and so was her smile. That seemed to charm Salamander immensely. He extended his meaty hand and automatically Sally grabbed it up and shook it.

His hand was slightly oily with moisture and his smile was sly and unctuous.

"My, my . . . and here is something that only humanity can attain," he said. His voice was richer this close and he seemed to savor it even as it trembled out of his lower registers. "True feminine beauty."

"Thank you!" said Sally.

Gad! What a *toad*. The politician smelled of lust. He was looking at her like some kind of rock star eyeing a groupie. It made Sally's skin crawl, but she had a mission here, so she responded with an eager, nonsuggestive smile.

"That's all very well, but I can see a rare intelligence in your eyes as well. . . . Certainly it takes smarts to appreciate the forthright but underappreciated wisdom of what I have to say!" he crowed.

Sheesh! thought Sally. *Modest fellow!*

"I really enjoyed your speech," she stated nonetheless, with an appropriate fawning expression. "I think it's a *wonderful* thing to be human. Living on an alien planet certainly makes me appreciate that."

"I should think so," said Salamander, patting her shoulder in a condescending manner. "I don't know how you do it! It's a hard thing here without the comforts of Earth. . . . The sweet smell of Mother Gaia's atmosphere . . . Fresh grass . . . Roses . . ."

"The New Jersey Turnpike," said Sally.

"Pardon?"

"The New Jersey Turnpike . . . my favorite smell. . . . It's got . . . well, a lived-in Nature scent. Like I tell those leftist environmentalists back home—what good is Nature to us if we don't *live* in it, *use* it . . . like God intended us to."

"Ah . . . Well, yes, of course. That could not be better said, Ms. . . ."

"Mrs. Please. I don't care for that silly word. I'm Mrs. Sally Brogan, and I'm proud to be my husband's wife . . ."

"Of course you are. . . ." said Salamander, clearly not totally pleased that she was a married woman—but not put off by it, either.

"No. Tell me how I can help. I really and truly think that we humans should stick together. Our interests and our rights are just as important as any other race in the Universe."

"Absolutely," said Salamander. "I can immediately see that you're just the kind of volunteer that we need. . . . So tell me, what brings you and your husband here to Demeter City?"

"Patrick—that's my husband—he's a policeman. He's here to help the Demeter Police with their crime problems. He's from New York City . . . and was one of the best cops back there."

"Ah . . . Yes. The Big Apple," said Salamander, grabbing up a cupcake well stacked with icing. "A transfer, I take it . . . A strange business . . . Giving away what it's taken us centuries to learn. And for what?" He unwrapped the cupcake delicately, then stuffed the entire thing into an enormous mouth. His cheeks bulged out like an enormous hamster's as he chewed. "An unfair trade, I think."

"I'm not sure my husband would agree with you, but I think I'm closer than he is to that point of view," said Sally diplomatically.

Boy, wait till Patrick gets a load of this guy.

Salamander grabbed himself a cup of coffee and slurped at it noisily, eyeing the stack of goodies, clearly deciding which one to take next. "Tell you what. I'm going to be involved personally with the kickoff meeting of our organization's chapter here on Demeter City. Right in this very spot. Why don't you come round early"—he winked at her conspiratorially—"and plan to stay late. You *could* have a very important part to play in a society of . . . let's face it . . . *intergalactic* importance."

She smiled but took a hasty half step away from him.

This smarmy Salamander guy was coming within a hairbreadth of patting her lasciviously on her behind.

"Thank you, Mister Salamander!" she said, grabbing up his chubby right hand and pumping it. "I'll do just that. Now, I *must* go off and buy one of your tapes for my family to listen to. And you must talk to your other admirers."

"Yes. I'll do that," said Salamander. "Perhaps I'll even have something special for you tomorrow night." He smiled. "Autographed."

Inwardly, Sally shuddered at the very thought. "That would be *wonderful*!" she said, smiling.

And then she got away from the guy.

CHAPTER 10

The Demeter night lay upon the city like a mysterious mask.

Fog slunk through streets and alleys, rising up off the central river and Lava Park in waves. Some of the Earthers who came here compared the place to what London must have been like in the diseased fogs of the nineteenth century. However, most agreed that the place was far stranger.

It wasn't just the smells here, the exotic spices, the strange mineral scents that wafted in the air, the odd fungoid sensory touches that were found in dank places like this. Nor was it the different colors, the shapes, the textures of the architecture, the lean of the buildings—all of which could be expected to be different on an alien planet.

No, that wasn't what bothered Joseph Salamander the most.

It was the *feel* of the place, the *energy* of the place. It had a spiritually bizarre flavor, and it made the politician yearn to be back in his familiar ranch style home in mid-America, eating his favorite meal: macaroni and cheese.

The more he got to know about alien planets, the more Salamander appreciated his native Earth, just as the more he'd gotten to know of foreign lands there, the more he appreciated his own Montana homeland and his own nation, his dear My Country 'Tis Of Thee, (sigh) the good ol' United States of America.

Mom.

Apple Pie.

Greenbacks.

All that made the Old Ways worth keeping New.

It gave him the creeps.

He didn't particularly like it now, waiting in this noisome alley for his contact. But then, here on Demeter City he didn't have the control he was used to.

Not yet, anyway.

A chill swept up his spine as a breeze whistled through the alley, carrying with it a few brightly colored wrappers.

He wrapped his coat tighter around him, pulling up his collar against the sudden change in temperature.

Something touched his shoulder.

He jumped.

Turned.

Standing there was a figure in a long dark robe, face totally covered by a long, draping hood.

Salamander took a few steps back, reaching

down for the gun he always kept concealed upon his person, even in church.

But he stopped.

"Scrunch?" he said.

"At your service," replied the figure.

"You really don't want to sneak up on me like that, Scrunch. We Earthers are a little nervous in strange places like this."

"As well you should be," said the robed being.

He pushed back the hood.

Standing there before Salamander was a very old Creon. His age was etched into his face in wrinkles that were more like fissures. However, his eyes were bright and strong, if mysterious, and there was a sturdy muscular presence in his stance.

Salamander relaxed a little, but held his defiant and prepared stance. This creature was an ally, but he was still an alien, and therefore, by definition, not necessarily to be one hundred percent trusted.

"I see by the televised news services that things are going along as planned," said Salamander, tentatively.

The Creon's bushy eyebrows rose questioningly. "Planned? When you deal with what we are dealing with, there are no *plans*."

His voice died into a whisper. "There is only *anarchy* and *mystery* . . . yes, and *fear*."

Salamander shivered. However, he did his best to conceal his own fear from the alien. Whether on Earth or otherwise, he well knew that it was the

Strong and the Strong-Willed that dominated and intimidated.

"Look, I don't pretend to know exactly how you're doing this. I don't know who you've employed to create the effects that I want, and I'm not sure I really *want* to know." He opened his coat and pulled out an envelope. "Here are the unmarked credit issues. Keep up the good work and you'll get more."

A rough-skinned hand reached out, lizardlike, and closed clawlike fingernails around the bulging envelope of notes. The arm hoisted them, brought them up before flat nostrils. Sniffed.

The mouth opened slightly in a smile to reveal a maw full of rotten teeth.

"Oh yes. Good work indeed," said the thing. "Just pray, sir, that the good work does not extend to you." The eyes glittered strangely, darkly. The voice croaked as though there were mystic gears grinding deep within.

"What are you talking about?"

"Who knows what forces we have set to work now, hmmm?" said the Creon. "A bit of this from the dark stars . . . a bit of that from our dark hearts."

"Look. When I contacted you people, all I asked was for you to help emphasize something that I already *know* to be true. This planet—the whole Universe—is *dangerous* to human beings. Back on my planet, this expansion to the stars thing is allowing far too much concentration to be placed on programs that are not in the best interest of my people. Liberal programs—not the conservative, considering ones that have allowed our people to become civilized, industrious, and wealthy and are in danger now of being forgotten in our silly enthusiasm to spread into a most-frightening future."

The eyebrow rose. "Save your speeches for your own species, politician," said Scrunch. "I have what I have done this for—and will continue to do what you wish—"

The Creon turned to leavc, his robe swishing up ground fog.

"Wait!" said Salamander.

The Creon stopped, turned around.

"You *will* be able to stop this thing, once our purpose is accomplished?"

"If that is indeed your wish," said the Creon.

"And what if I need particular . . . ah . . . *humans* . . . dealt with."

The Creon held up his hands. "You need but say the word!

Again, the creepy ruined smile . . . and then the alien turned and was swallowed by the fog.

Salamander got the hell out of there.

CHAPTER 11

"Well," said Took. "Here you have just about everything you could possibly want—just at the tinkle of a bell."

She spread her arms in a welcoming way, gesturing out to the beautiful house that was all theirs. The place was situated on the outskirts of Demeter City, on a slight rise, and afforded an absolutely breathtaking view of that splendorous city. On one side was a river, and on the other a field. The house itself was surrounded by a wall, with security emplacements. Anything approaching could be seen from a long way off.

Now, as Officer Jack Haldane looked out upon the sight of the morning fog slowly being evaporated by the sun that had only recently pushed itself from the horizon, he was not feeling particularly secure or particularly happy.

He gazed over at Officer Jane Castle.

She was back in uniform now, looking trim and fit and businesslike. No makeup to speak of, no smile. Doing her duty. As attractive and perky as ever, though. In normal situations, this would be a splendid opportunity. Time with Jane! Date duty! Alas, there was another little detail involved here. . . .

"Blatt! Blatt!"

What *was* it with that *word?*

Yanx seemed obsessed with it.

First thing this morning, soon as he was hauled into this place, it was "Blatt" this or "Blatt" that. Didn't the little guy get tired of it?

There he was now, crawling alongside one of the couches in the huge room. Totally out of control as usual. One of the Tarn nurses who had been hired to watch him asked him politely to sit and be still. Yanx ignored her. These nurses came in shifts, one for every eight hours—but because of their supposed special psychic ability to "protect" Yanx in tandem, he and Jane were stuck there twenty-five hours a day! (More or less. . . . A day's length shifted around on this planet . . . but it suited Jack Haldane's circadian rhythms to a T.)

"A little ball of energy, isn't he?" said Jane tartly, clearly not quite as fond of the tyke as she had been originally. The notion of dealing with a crawling baby for an indefinite period of time while waiting for something almost supernatural was slightly more daunting than merely cooing at him from a distance. "I'm sure you'll get along just fine." She went over and patted the crawling baby on the head. "Now you be good, little one!"

"Blatt!" said Yanx, holding up his arms, looking cute and entreating.

"Okay, okay," said Took.

She picked him up.

A big smile of pleasure passed over the baby's face.

"He seems to be doing well, even without his mom and dad here," said Haldane hopefully.

"Momma!" said Yanx, pointing at Haldane, a big grin angling up toward his ears.

Castle laughed.

"Kid, *I'm* not your momma!" said Haldane. "Besides, where did 'Blatt' go?"

The child looked puzzled.

"I thought you *hated* Blatt," said Castle.

Yanx's eyes tracked along to the speaker. He pointed, eyes lighting up again.

"Dadda!" he said, pointing at Jane.

"A little confusion, I'm sure," said Took, handing the baby over to the Tarn nurse. "However, perhaps it's fortunate for the time being. Who knows how long it will be before he'll be able to see his real parents?"

"It's just fortunate that's even going to be possible," said Jane.

"Yes, indeed," said Took. "Well, now. Radio contact is at your fingertips." She gestured outside. "We've got enough armed guards to man a citadel, with all the modern weapons possible. Lasers, guns of all variety. I'd say this is about as safe as you can possibly be—"

"I still would have preferred to be up in orbit," said Jack. "I'd feel much more secure there."

"Ah yes, and so you would . . . but then, that's not the main point, is it—" She pointed down to a group of lab-coated Tarn and Creon scientist-sorts. They were huddled around a peculiar device that looked like a radar scope mated with an antenna far on the extreme side of abstract art. "You have several of the finest minds in electromagnetic sentience down there, ready to trap this creature . . . and naturally hoping that it will show up."

"Which is why Yanx is here. . . ." said Jane.

"And we're here in case all that modern equipment doesn't work," added Jack.

"Precisely. Now, I have to get back to Headquarters," said Took, walking away briskly. "But I'll be sure to check in regularly. And don't ever be afraid to consult with me about absolutely *anything*."

"Diapers?" said Jack.

"Fortunately, that's not your duty," said Took.

She bade farewell and was soon gone.

A moment of silence descended upon them.

Jack Haldane rocked on his heels a moment, sucking a tooth. There was a distinct feel of uneasiness in the air. . . .

"Well . . ." said Jane. "I don't suppose I could talk you into a game of dominoes?"

"You brought them along?"

"Sure. And a few other games."

"Games? At a time like this?"

"You haven't seen the movies?"

"What movies?"

"Twentieth-century movies. All the cops play games at stakeouts."

"This is a stakeout?"

"Well, not exactly—same principle, though. People sitting around, waiting for something to happen."

"I don't know if you've noticed it or not—but something *is* happening."

He pointed at Yanx.

Yanx was struggling in the nurse's hands, staring at one of his playthings in the corner, no doubt trying to get at it.

"Go ahead. He won't hurt anything," said Jane.

The nurse let Yanx down and the youngster eagerly crawled toward the pile of toys, like some whirlwind force of nature unleashed.

"True, but that's what the nurse and the playthings are for."

Jane turned to the nurse. "Besides, it's not like you're going to be extremely active for a while."

"Hey! I can still walk."

"Yes, perhaps . . . rather like the Frankenstein monster, don't you think?" She winked at him. "Look, why don't you just make it easy on yourself? If I have to be cooped up in a house with you and a Tarn baby, I'll be a whole lot happier if I can regularly whomp you in games."

"Hey! Who said you would win?"

"That's the spirit!"

"I may not be ace at dominoes, but try me at card games!"

"Oh, most certainly!" Her brow furrowed, then lightened.

"What do you say to a small wager?"

"Wager? Like in money?"

"Yes!"

"Maybe," he thought furiously. Then smiled. "Tell you what. We're together here, and I don't mind that at all."

"I didn't really think you would. . . ."

"But we never finished up properly on Saturday night, and besides . . . from the very start, all you could squawk about was how it 'really wasn't a date.' Well, I'll tell you what, Ms. Jane Castle. We'll play a series of games . . . Card games, mind you. Or heck . . . even checkers."

"Oh, let's not get *too* advanced."

". . . we play those games . . . at the end of this, we tally up points. If I get the most points . . . I get a *real* date with you . . . and you have to be cordial and nice to me."

Jane blanched. "Oh dear. That's quite the prize! Thank goodness you haven't a prayer of achieving it." Her eyes lit. "Okay then . . . what do I get?"

"A date with me . . . and you can be as mean and derisive as you always are . . . wait . . . even more so if you like!" He smiled.

"You think you're *so* clever, don't you?"

"Sometimes."

"If afraid it's *not* going to work. No—if . . . or should I say *when* I win . . . you have to promise me that you won't make any propositions, any proposals . . . You won't make any lewd suggestion or innuendo . . . And you most certainly won't keep on asking me *out*! Let's see . . . for say, six months."

"Sheesh. Torture!"

"Four."

"Two."

"Three. That's my last offer . . . besides, you won't have to worry at all if you're really all that good at games, hmm?"

"I am if I'm not dominoed!"

"Indeed, indeed. Three months of peace. That would be my price . . . and my prize."

Haldane shrugged as best he could under his conditions.

"Okay. Negotiations over. I'll play with you."

"Oh *good*. I might actually *enjoy* this." She went over to the side of the room to rummage through the supplies.

"Let me see. What's your feeling on War?"

"I'm a pacifist."

"No, no, the *card* game!"

"Oh . . . isn't that a little too *difficult?*" She was rummaged through a pile. "Where's that deck? I knew it was in here somewhere."

"Ha ha. Concentration, then?"

"I've got Attention Deficit Disorder."

"Old Maid."

"Look, really, let's be serious here . . . we're going to have to choose a card game of *some* adult character."

"Poker?"

"With *two* people?"

"Maybe the nurse wants to play."

"Be real, Haldane."

"Maybe Yanx . . . Yeah, he could have a stash of money somewhere and we can win it off him."

"I don't think so."

"Well . . . hmmm. I'm good at anything except bridge . . . So what do you say to gin rummy?"

"Gin is a good two-people game," allowed Jane. She moved a backgammon box to one side, then a chess and Parcheesi set. "Where *are* the cards?"

Something caught Jack Haldane's drifting gaze. He turned and he saw Yanx, cooing and playing in the corner, just as he was supposed to be.

Something, though, was odd about this picture.

There was something floating above the kid. Haldane stepped closer and he saw what it was.

A pack of cards.

"Ah—Jane . . . Don't look now, but I do believe that Yanx *would* like to play."

Jane turned and smiled. "Oh . . . There they are! So we have a little cardsharp here, then, hmmm?" She stepped forward, holding out her hand. "Could you please give those to me, dear? Uncle Jack and I would like to use them."

"*Uncle?* I thought I was 'Mommy,'" said Jack.

"Give them here, Yanx. Be a good boy!" said Jane.

She started over, holding her hand out.

Pure delight showed on Yanx's face.

"Blatt!" he cried out.

The cards exploded.

For a brief moment there was a cloud of them in the air, and then they fluttered down, flopping onto Jane's head and clacking onto the floor.

Yanx let loose a squeal of joy, pointing at Jane.

"Say! I know a good one," said Jack Haldane. "Fifty-two Pickup!"

Officer Jane Castle did not look thrilled.

CHAPTER 12

She looked about thirty years old.

Auburn hair, deep brown eyes, a full mouth, and a body that just wouldn't quit, even in the no-nonsense blues of the Demeter Police uniform that she wore now.

"Lieutenant Brogan," said Captain Podly. "This is your new partner for the interim . . . Officer Christina Fleur."

Brogan shook her hand. It was warm and soft and she gripped his with a soothing firmness. "Hello, Officer Fleur."

"Please, call me Chris."

She had a trace of an accent. French? Whatever it was, her voice was sultry and evocative. It stirred forgotten embers in Brogan's cusp-of-middle-aged mind.

Warm embers.

"Officer Fleur is a new transfer from the European Central Police on Earth," said Podly. "She's been in school the past few years and has been absorbing everything so quickly, she is the obvious temporary replacement for Officer Haldane."

"Oh. Well, you've got some big shoes to fill."

She looked at him with a penetrating stare, a sarcastic tilt to her head. "Size isn't necessarily of importance—in most matters, anyway." She stood tall and proud, looking absolutely confident that she could deal with anything that came her way, alien or otherwise. She gave Brogan the once-over, as though sizing him up for herself. "I hope you'll find me quite capable, Lieutenant. In any case, I do not pretend to be anything more than your assistant and student. Although I hope to bring what experience and learning I have to the task at hand."

Podly dipped those incredible large eyes at Brogan in a "See why I chose this one" kind of way. "And there is quite the task at hand, I think."

"Thank you for fully apprising me of the situation, this morning, Captain Podly." She pulled out a disk from her side pocket, brandished it knowingly. "You may be sure that I have fully assimilated this information and am ready to operate."

Podly looked extremely pleased. "What's your take on the whole thing, Lieutenant, from your study?"

In truth, what with all the excitement of the weekend, along with family matters, Brogan hadn't been able to more than browse through the material. However, he was a New York cop, and he was used to breezing through the bureaucracy.

"I've got a few leads I intend to check out. Excellent stuff there, Captain. Very helpful."

Podly nodded, mollified.

RULE #4: When bullshitting, praise your superior's work.

"Officer Fleur has been acquainted with the details of the attack and of what little we know about the creature. She also shows a splendid grasp of both Creon and Tarn psychobiology."

"And may I add, my minor in college was xenobiology," she said. "A field that has, in the last few years, broadened immensely."

"And what was your major, Officer Fleur?"

"A double major, Lieutenant. Chemistry and political science."

"Quite a science background then. How did that lead to police work?"

"The European police are quite modern. There was an opening in a lab. I became fascinated with police work and I excelled. When I had the opportunity to deal with xenobiology firsthand—you can, of course, understand that I grabbed it immediately with great enthusiasm." Her eyes seemed to glow with passion. Brogan realized that his heart was beating a little faster.

This was going to be an interesting partner, for sure.

He just hoped she wouldn't be too interesting.

"Excellent," said Podly. "I look forward very much to your report at the end of the day. It should shed a great deal more light on the situation. Now then, Brogan. I know you've got your own network of informants to deal with these things—but this little tidbit just came up this morning. I want you to go down immediately and check it out before you do anything else."

He handed Brogan a sheet.

Brogan read it out loud. "The All-Seeing Chapel of the Cosmic Wanderer?"

"Yes, that's right. Slomo did another run of possiblities with the material on file, and that popped up as high-probability."

"It has associations with this supposed cult we're looking for, I take it," said Officer Fleur.

"Good call. A smart one, isn't she, Lieutenant?" said Podly, and for the first time Brogan wondered if maybe sex appeal wasn't an interspecies phenomenon.

"She seems to have plenty on the ball. It will be good to work with you, Chris."

"Likewise."

"Yes, that possible cult. You have the address. You've been introduced. So what are you waiting for! Get to work."

However brusque, Captain Podly was smiling grimly as he said it.

"It's a beautiful descent," said Officer Christina Fleur as the hopper pierced the atmosphere and quickly headed down toward Demeter City on its wild ride on the Gravity Train from the Space Precinct.

"Yeah. This is quite the planet. Have you had a chance for a tour of its natural wonders?"

"Frankly, no. I've been so busy since I've gotten here with orientation and training, I've hardly had the time for anything leisurely."

"Doesn't look like you're going to have time now, either. They've plunged you into the Unnatural Wonders of Demeter City headfirst."

"I'm doing this happily. I am absolutely fascinated with the idea of some sort of being that seems to be half-material and half-energy . . . able to shift back and forth so easily. There's nothing like it on Earth. . . . And we've barely been able to speculate silicon-based life among the stars, much less this."

There seemed true spirit to this woman, and it was even more attractive than her outer accoutrements.

If he were a single man . . . thought Brogan.

Now now, he admonished himself. *Down, boy. You're married and very happily married.*

Fortunately, he had to attend to the details of deceleration and could concentrate on more immediate things.

The cityscape of the megalopolis was abruptly upon them, and even though he'd seen it many times before, Brogan couldn't help but be impressed by the rising towers, the strange catwalks and byways, the air of Big Town Meets Alien that Demeter City exuded.

Christina Fleur was clearly overwhelmed.

"I've been here a few times before, but it still gets to me," she explained after a few moments of awe as they swooped in among the towers.

"Oh yeah," said Brogan. "I know exactly what you mean."

They found the Police Substation, and changed to a cruiser. Brogan couldn't help noticing the eyes of the few men there dart toward Christina.

A human mechanic named Al was working on the cruiser. When he had a look at her, his eyes got big. "Hello, hello. Brogan, looks like you traded in Haldane for a sleeker model. Though that wouldn't be difficult."

Introductions were made.

"How's she doing?" said Brogan, nodding to the cruiser.

"She'll hold up," said the squat, older Al. He chomped on some gum. "I wouldn't chase anything at light speed or go around corners too quickly, though. I think I've got some more work to do on the differential and the equalizer."

"Work? Al, I need to be able to TRUST my vehicle."

"Hey . . . Excuse me, huh? I'm doin' my best! And it ain't as though we've exactly got these high-powered numbers comin' outta our ears. You want top performance, you gotta take some time . . .

And we don't get NO time here in Auto Bay!"

"Okay, okay, I'm sure it'll be fine. We're in a hurry, anyway."

"Yeah, well hurry and come back, Officer Fleur. I gotta hot cup of espresso waitin' just for you." He winked at her.

In the cruiser, heading toward their destination, Christina said, "Are all the men in this precinct so forward?"

"There aren't a great number of single women out here. . . . And I suspect that even if there were, Chris, you'd have an impact on them."

"That's very nice, but I really haven't got time for that kind of thing. I'm pretty much dedicated to my work here. Maybe that's why I already feel comfortable with you, Lieutenant. You're a married man, I understand."

"You bet."

"Good. It's just business between us then."

"Absolutely."

"Mostly, that is," she said. "I don't want to seem unfriendly at all."

"Don't worry about it. And one warning . . . if you meet my regular partner?"

"Oh yes. Officer Haldane."

"Watch out. Although right now he does have his eyes on someone else. Although I strongly suspect that after the next few days they won't be speaking to each other."

"That's all immaterial to me. I'm simply keen on doing my job here . . . and extremely curious as to what we're facing."

"Curious is healthy here . . . Too curious isn't . . . And let me tell you, a little bit of fear and caution doesn't hurt, either."

"Naturally." She nodded. "I think that we'll be a good team . . . Matt."

"Okay, Chris. Who gets to be the bad cop?"

"Oh. Please." She smiled mischievously. "Me!"

"No. You look like an angel. I'll be the bad cop today."

She laughed. "Okay, if that's what you want." She pointed at the screen on the console of the cruiser. "I took the liberty of programming in our destination."

"Yep. I noticed your efficiency . . . and, from the looks of things, I'd say that we're almost there."

They'd passed an area of sleek towers and verdant parks and now were in less pleasant territory. These were older areas with grungy buildings and humps of things that were supposed to be buildings, but seemed more like decomposing mushrooms with the occasional window. Streets cut through this fungoid vision like a hasty afterthought. What citizens there were seemed to prefer traveling in automated vehicles: there were virtually no pedestrians.

"I don't think that you have to explain to me that this is the less well-to-do part of town," said Christina, after studying it all both through the windows and on a viewer.

"This is the Mluck District. It may rhyme with 'luck,' but its fate has never much been in that direction," said Brogan. "The nearest analog I can think of is the South Bronx before the 2020 Borough Renaissance programs."

"Yes, I have seen documentaries concerning that area of your New York City. It does have that bombed-out look to it. Gutted. A shame, for I detect a great deal of interesting architecture here."

"Yes, it was built by immigrants from the planet Ardant," said Brogan. "The Ardentians were one of the original partners in building the Demeter City we know now. However, for some reason they lost interest in their enterprise, and for the most part went back to their home planet. Only a few remain in Demeter City—and most of them are here in what's left of their principal area."

The viewer beeped, then performed a series of screen changes, culminating in a square being pointed at by an arrow, with an address blinking at the bottom.

"That's the place," said Brogan. "Let's take her down, shall we?"

Christina looked very serious. "Yes. I'm ready."

Brogan took the cruiser down, sliding it into a narrow alley. Its jets blew up trash as it landed. When it touched down, and Brogan turned off the engines, an eerie silence folded in on them.

"Feels rather deserted, doesn't it?" said Christina, not sounding particularly frightened, but not sounding at all thrilled about getting out into the odd scene that surrounded them now.

"Yes. What you'd call 'preternaturally still,' I suppose."

Up this close, the odd, alien building not only appeared ramshackle and rotting, but actually decomposing and oozing. Brogan wasn't sure if this was part of the original artistry of the buildings. Now, though, it certain lent everything a decidedly creepy air. The Ardentians didn't seem to have much in the way of a concept of a straight line. And if things were supposed to blend together organically, then it was a definitely skewed set of organs. Lights pulsed faintly here and there in queasy shades of green and purple, and tendrils of fleshy type matter hung in the doorway like absent-minded curtains.

When he opened the door, Brogan was also reminded of another unfortunate aspect of the Ardentian area.

Its smell wasn't particularly pleasant.

The aroma here was rather like old tennis shoes, mold, and dead river sludge.

Christina's nostrils cringed a bit, but she bore the stench like a trouper, not even commenting. She had the amazing quality European women sometimes had, a combination of eroticism and reserve, of sexiness and sophistication, edged by a knowing mystery. American women generally were much more up-front about things, and Brogan preferred that, actually. However, the European quality certainly piqued his imagination.

"There it is," she said, pointing at a sludge of light spilling out from a nest of protuberances at one side of what could loosely be termed a building.

"Very good," said Brogan. "Yes, that must be it. You read the computer very well . . ."

She shrugged. "A good sense of direction, a healthy dose of intuition—plus, of course, this is the only spread of lights in the area."

Brogan smiled. "Always a good clue." As they approached the lights, he noticed hieroglyphics painstakingly painted on the side of the building in an ornate and illuminated manner worthy of the monks of the Middle Ages. He squinted to read them. "Can't quite make out—Hmm."

"Not Creon or Tarn writing, that's for sure," said Christina as they neared.

"Well . . . You *have* been learning. I must admit, I'm not much of a scholar on either."

"Both are more flowing. These are block letters with no space. Not a difficult observation." She looked at him. "Ardentian?"

"That would be the logical deduction, although there are certainly *other* forms of intelligent life with writing on Demeter City."

"There's only one way of finding out." She examined the opening at the door. "Does one knock in such circumstances?"

"I'm not sure that will do much good, but it seems the polite thing to do." Brogan stepped up and raised his fist to begin rapping.

"Wait. There's some sort of button there. A door buzzer?"

"A universal concept, apparently." Brogan pressed it. Some kind of jangling noise like inverted chimes resulted.

There was no immediate response.

Brogan was about to attempt the knocking method, but stopped as a door opened.

The being inside the building was backlit in murky color-shaded shadows and was the most astonishing alien Patrick Brogan had seen for a while.

CHAPTER 13

"Welcome to our humble temple," said the being. "My name is Kawkor. We provide enlightenment and answers to age-old questions—at highly affordable rates!"

"Well, thanks, but we're here on official business," said Brogan. "This is Officer Christina Fleur. I'm Lieutenant Patrick Brogan. We're from the Demeter City Police Force."

The creature nodded. "Ah yes. That most welcome addition to this fair city after years of chaos and Anarchy." Its voice was soft, soothing, and comforting.

Its looks were quite another matter.

Brogan couldn't help but notice Christina jump when the thing first appeared, and he didn't blame her at all.

The cowl and robe that it wore were about the only things remotely familiar about the creature.

Its body looked like a lumpy pile from some junkyard, with angular protrusions jutting and bumps humping that gave the thing absolutely no aesthetic lines or appeal whatsoever. Its face looked like nothing so much as a bunch of sausages loosely tied together at one end and allowed to splay out at the other.

In short, it was incredibly ugly.

"We need to ask you some questions," said Christina.

"May we come in?" added Brogan. Not because he particularly wanted to, but because he thought that there might be some kind of clue or information apparent in the interior.

"But of course. You must be aware, however, that there is a *baxa* meditation class in session," said the alien.

"We shall be as quiet as possible," said Brogan.

"Oh, quiet is not necessary," said Kawkor. "However, I *would* encourage caution."

Some kind of limp appendage rose up from its robes and beckoned them inward. Brogan and Fleur exchanged apprehensive glances, but followed.

The temperature inside was much cooler. It had the feel of a damp cavern or sepulcher, planted with some exotic garden. It was not an unpleasant odor, thought Brogan. However, like many of the other interior odors on Demeter City, it had nothing to do with anything Earthly or familiar and, therefore, by its very nature, made him feel nervous.

They were led down a narrow passage that dipped on a severe incline to a lower level that opened up into a huge chamber, filled with all sorts of things, including the promised meditation class, sitting on stools in a group to the left. The class was made entirely of Tarns and Creons, and they all wore simple white pajama type clothing, rather like Oriental martial arts *gis*. Beside them were piles of rags and oddments. In front of them was a hooded fellow, droning some kind of chant in a grating, racheting voice.

"I take it that's the *baxa* class," said Christina.

"I would think so. . . . I didn't realize this cult had an educational system."

"That would explain the association."

"Association?'

"Yes. The murdered alien. I've read the notes."

"Yeah. Of course."

He had to remember that Christina probably knew as much as he did, if not more, about this whole case. She was exactly the type to be up to speed, and Brogan felt a sense of anxiety and competition. It was almost as if this woman wanted his job—It was a strange feeling here on Demeter City, but one he was well aware of back home in the hustle of New York. Hell, he'd probably given that uneasy feeling to his superiors when *he* was young.

"Welcome to our humble temple," said the alien, gesturing with an attempt to be expansive with its limbs, but failing miserably. "Please feel at home."

There was absolutely nothing that would make Brogan feel at home in this place. It had a roundish dome shape and "rooms" were marked off in gradations of levels, some with steps, some simply jutting out from the side of the stone walls. The largest of these rooms had some kind of altar arrangement, with pewlike slabs in front. The other smaller "rooms" held different amounts of furniture and displays of pictures and idols. Some of the levels were occupied by hooded monks. One was filled with cages containing monkeylike creatures. One held a fanged, striped beast chained to a post. All in all, the whole room looked more like an odd ring in an odder circus than a temple. But then, of course, it was an alien temple of an alien religion on an alien planet with no drive to conform to any of *his* prejudices as to what temples should be like, thought Brogan. He had to remind himself of one of the key lessons he'd learned on Demeter City: Don't make assumptions.

Brogan took a moment to look around. Offhand he could see nothing that could offer any help in the case. Certainly none of the idols or pictures resembled the creature that had attacked the Tarn concert hall.

"Thanks for your help. We have a few questions for you." From his pocket, he pulled out pictures of the dead Creon.

Before and After.

He showed them to the monk.

"We have reason to believe that this citizen of Demeter City was a member of your cult."

"Cult? Cult?" said Kawkor. "Please! From my studies of your culture—and yes, we count ourselves nothing if not scholars of all cultures, all information and texts that flow into this amazing focal point that is Demeter City—from my reading I would assume that your connotation of 'cult' does not place our universal views in a particularly positive light."

"No offense. We just want to get information," said Brogan.

"We need to guard the well-being of not merely the citizens of Demeter City, but the citizens of the galaxy," said Christine, voice ringing with self-assurance and virtue. Brogan felt buoyed by her self-assurance and wished he could be self-possessed in these matters himself. Podly was right. This new officer was working out just fine.

"I am aware of preconceptions you might have—" said the creature. Its voice was smooth and comforting, and the sausages that composed its face stirred in a way that might have been an alien smile. "However, please be reassured: We do not worship violent gods, we have no threatening esoteric practices and we do not sacrifice virgins or any other species of living being upon bloody altars."

Normally in these circumstances, Brogan would have stared into a suspect's eyes in order to register any kind of pupil dilation or what-have-you that would signify a prevarication.

However, since Brogan didn't know where the hell this thing's eyes *were*, that chore was rather difficult.

There *were* little shiny dots on the ends of the sausages.

Organic photoelectric sensors?

Perhaps. But then, with aliens, you couldn't assume anything. Like the time he'd shot that criminal and killed him by mistake, because he hadn't known that its brain was under its arm.

"That's all well and good, and I'm sure that you even hold decent Sunday school classes," said Brogan. "Only let's get around to my question. Do you know this Creon?"

"Pardon me. My narrative abilities often sweep me up in their resonance and enunciative powers," said the alien. A crooked thing it used for a limb snaked from its robe and bent fingers closed around the photos.

Brogan watched intently as it brought them up to its "face" and pored over them intently—with what, however, Brogan was not exactly certain.

"Ah yes. Tark Norgal," said the alien. "Certainly; he took many of our classes. He even recently officially joined our fellowship. However, he was never particularly a fiercely devoted acolyte."

"He was a businessman," said Christina.

"Ah yes. That's right. He owned a store . . . and I believe that store recently fell upon hard times. I know that because we allowed his tithing to be suspended because of his financial difficulties. No, we are not a particularly hard-nosed bunch! Not at all!"

Nosed? thought Brogan. He didn't see any noses on them at all!

"Be that as it may, your guy here was horribly murdered under extremely unusual circumstances," said Christina. She tapped the "After" picture, showing Tark Nargal in his state of extreme disrepair.

"Yes. Believe me, we are aware of that—we are neither hard-nosed nor cold-hearted. Services for our departed Brother were held just the other night. His spirit now mingles with our incense here, and rises slowly to bask in the righteousness of the All within Even More."

The alien made some kind of symbolic gesture with another limb.

"Perhaps you can answer a few questions then," said Brogan, distracted despite himself by the nearby mediators, who now seemed to be involved with some kind of jerky conniption dance. Their chanting drone had turned less regular and contained squeaks and squawks. Even the atmosphere seemed to have turned slightly more sour, if possible.

There was more agitation in the air, certainly, and Brogan could tell that Christina sensed it as well.

The monk, however, registered no changes or acknowledgments of the situation at all.

"Please! Ask away! That is why I have invited you down here. Indeed, it is my prayer that you will allow me to bestow upon you some of our literature, that you might understand our spiritual system and communicate it to your fellow humans."

Suddenly Brogan found a handful of brochures stuffed into his face.

"That's not why we're here," said Christina.

"I'm afraid my partner is right," said Brogan. "However, I will take your reading matter." He reached up and took the pamphlets. They were written in Creon, but he could barely translate them. Something about "Light" and "Saved by."

"Ah! Excellent. Thank you so much. You have made my day!" said the monk. His sausages waved enthusiastically. "Now then, what more can I tell you?"

"That's what we were hoping you'd tell us," said Brogan. "Let's start off with *your* association with the victim."

"None! Passing reference. I believe he was in one of my consecration classes. That's all."

"Did you see him on the night of his death?"

"Absolutely not. And we have no records of Tark Nargal being anywhere near this building for *days* before his unfortunate demise," said the Brother.

"In your pantheon of gods and demons—"

"Please. Spiritual beings."

"Ah yes. In your realm of spiritual beings, is there any creature that is both energy, spirit, and matter and preys upon the energies of others?"

"Hmmm. Well, there's Brpppppt, quasi deity of plumbing. And Strapp, demigoddess of swamp gas—but no, nothing quite like you describe. . . ."

"Liar!" cried a voice from the class.

One of the Creons was standing. His large eyes were wide and bloodshot.

"Tell them! We're doomed. All *doomed!*"

From his cloak he pulled out a huge knife, and then raced, shrieking, toward them.

CHAPTER 14

"Gin!" said Jack Haldane.

He slapped his cards down with happy finality.

"Here. Take your hand away and let me have a look," said Jane Castle.

"Sure."

Jack grinned with great self-satisfaction. This twenty-some points would put him within easy reach of the hundred necessary to win this game.

A *true* date with Jane Castle would then not be far away at all.

She looked at his cards, all of which matched up perfectly, and then threw down her own with disgust. "I can't believe it! You actually *are* good at this game."

"And you didn't believe me."

"Doomed," she moaned mournfully. "Doomed!"

Haldane scooped the cards up and folded them together into a stack for the next deal. Playing cards with a cast was not as hard as he thought it might be. "Game's not over yet, Castle. Besides—you might actually enjoy yourself."

"What? Enjoy losing to you? I think not!"

"No. Enjoy our date?"

She watched cannily as he shuffled. "Assuming this hyperhypothetical date occurs . . . If I *don't* enjoy myself . . . as I strongly suspect will be the case . . . If I *don't* enjoy myself, do I have to pretend?"

"You mean, like *fake* it?"

"I believe that is the gauche term, yeah."

"What would the difference be?" said Haldane, fanning the cards together briskly and smugly.

"What's that supposed to mean?"

"I mean, we've spent a great deal of time together and you *pretend* not to enjoy it very much, when in fact, I strongly sense that you're often in total rapture in my presence."

"Of all the . . ." She seemed truly incensed, and Haldane enjoyed it. "The extent of your arrogance astonishes me. Whatever gave you that idea?"

Haldane paused long enough from his cards to tap his nose.

"Do your nostrils itch?" she asked, piqued.

"No. My nose. . . . It gave you away!"

"Your *nose*? What kind of maniac are you, Jack Haldane?"

"An olfactory maniac, Jane."

"What?"

"When you're around me, you give off the most aromatic pheromones. The nose knows. This ole factory keeps working all the time!"

"Manufacturing exactly *what* the civilized mind boggles at!"

"Many civilized women have reported that yours truly can boggle quite well!" He pushed the cards her way. "Care to cut?"

"When within weapon's distance from you, Haldane, far too often. I will maintain the peace, however, by splitting the stack in half and recombining—a necessary move when playing cards with a boggler, I'm sure."

Smugly, Jack Haldane took the deck and dealt out ten cards apiece. He turned up the knock card. A five of clubs. Then he examined his hand. Two pairs and the beginnings of a straight.

This looked very good indeed.

The play commenced in earnest.

Jane Castle was totally focused. A pink tip of tongue showed from the side of her mouth as she rearranged her cards in their optimum order.

Cards were picked up, cards were discarded.

A nine of hearts was a welcome companion to his other nines. . . .

Jane smiled as she picked up a card from the main pile.

"Well. There, that's more like it."

"Hmm. I'd hardly call that a poker face," admonished Haldane.

"We're playing gin . . . Oops . . . Perhaps I shouldn't have reminded you."

"Yes. Horrible strategy."

"Jack—You know, we'd really get along much better if you behaved yourself."

"I keep my hands to myself."

"No, no . . . I mean, your ego. Just relax, okay? If we have to spend time together, maybe it would be best to just play it cool, hmm?"

"Okay. I'm cool. I still want to win that date, though.

"And you'll have a good time on it, whether you like it or not!"

His eyes glared empathically at her.

"Not in your bloody life!" Her nostrils flared. She was clearly incensed.

Good. It might spoil her play.

He picked up a couple more cards in the straight. Too many points yet to knock. That was okay, though. All he needed was another three and it was gin city. . . .

He reached for the next card.

In his gut, he could feel it was the one he wanted—

From the other room, there came a crashing and clattering, a tumult of catastrophic proportions.

Carefully, Haldane put his cards facedown upon the table. When you were this close to winning, you didn't want to foul up the game.

Jane Castle put hers down as well, but not so carefully.

"We'd better go have a look, hmmm?"

"Doesn't sound as though we're being attacked," said Haldane, moving with grace and ease toward the other room. "Sounded more like a baby boom to me."

Jane Castle looked as though, in less stressful

times, she might have made some sort of comment on that figure of speech. However, now they were both busily speeding toward the other room.

The sight met their noses before it met their eyes. There was the distinct scent of spilled aromatics in the air: perfume and cologne and all manner of other scents.

The sight itself was what they'd expected: a mild disaster entirely of Yanx's devising. There were smashed bottles scattered willy-nilly everywhere. Yanx's nurse hid, terrified, behind a couch. The security officers had exited the room and were peering in, looking to see if the coast was clear.

"Blatt!" said Yanx, and a flower-shaped bottle rocketed upward, exploding on the ceiling in a tinkling cataclysm. A fine mist of rosy scent veiled down slowly.

"In all my days, I've not seen a more telekinetically gifted child," said the nurse, shaking her head. "It's very hard indeed to handle him!"

"Must be because his parents aren't around," said a Tarn security officer.

"This kid's been mischievous as long as *I've* known him," said Brogan.

"Yanx," said Jane, holding her arms out. "Come here, and quit this ridiculousness!"

"What happened?" said Haldane.

"Well, he was playing quite peacefully with the fuzz-extravaganza toy." The nurse pointed at an odd, ovoid device with varicolored feathery extrusions. "I must admit I thought it was safe to peruse a book I brought with me. However, the next thing

I knew, he'd gotten a door open—and discovered a treasure trove of bottles."

"And immediately you just *had* to start playing with them, didn't you, you cute little devil," said Jane, cautiously approaching him, hand still extended.

"Don't compliment him," said Haldane. "You'll only encourage the little monster."

"Blatt!" said the little Tarn.

However, no further full bottles—and Haldane could see quite a few of them, displayed in their rainbow finery on the shelves—flew.

"You'd think a little variation in his vocabulary might help with his self-esteem." said Haldane.

"Please," said Jane. "He might get ahold of 'Splat'!"

Delight registered on the Tarn baby's cherubic face.

"Splat! Splat! Splat!"

"Oh dear," said Jane. "Perhaps I should have spelled it out. Come here. Be a good little boy and let your Aunt Jane give you a hug."

"Aunt Jane. Sounds positively spinsterish!" said Haldane. "I'd take care of that soon, if I were you."

"Splat! Splat!" said Yanx. And, quite prophetically, one more "SPLAT."

This time Yanx's little third eye opened wider than Haldane had ever seen it open before.

Five large bottles of colored liquid floated up from the closet shelves. They hovered for a moment—

"Yanx! No!"

—then smashed together.

Glass pieces fell onto the floor.

The liquid splashed down in a shower of droplets. However, in mixing, they caused strange, greenish clouds of gas that sparkled and glowed ominously.

"Blatt?" said Yanx, tremulously and uncertainly.

The cloud passed like a slow wave over the nurse, who coughed and almost immediately fainted.

"Get her out of here!" Haldane ordered the security guards.

Coughing themselves, the guards grabbed the nurse and hauled her out of the room.

"Grab him, Jane," said Haldane, stepping back himself.

Jane Castle dipped down and hauled Yanx up, carrying him away.

The cloud advanced.

"Wait a minute. That thing could mess up this entire environment," said Haldane. "We'd get chased out of here and be in *plenty* of trouble . . ." He turned to Yanx. "Kid! Look there! You've made a *horrible* mess. It's *bad* . . ."

"Oh dear," said Jane. "Do you really think you ought to challenge his boundaries on this. . . ."

"It's our only hope," said Haldane.

Yanx was frowning. He turned and pointed a pudgy finger at the expanding gas. His little nose wrinkled. "Bad!"

"Yes, Yanx, yes. Bad! Can you make it go away?"

"Bad!" said Yanx, and his third eyelid quivered. Frowning even deeper, he stared intently at the billowing gas . . .

The change was almost immediately noticeable.

The gas started to roll back. From its large consuming mass it withdrew slowly into a dense ball that slid back inside the closet. The harsh smell immediately diminished.

"Good! Yanx, very good!" piped Jane.

"Good!" parroted Yanx. "Good."

"You bet, kid. Thanks. Take him in the other room while I see about a detail to take care of this mess before it spreads any farther," said Haldane.

"Sure. Come on, little one. Let's go in and have some juice and a serious discussion."

"Splat," said Yanx, happy again.

"No. I'll not have any splats this time, all right?" said Jane as she carried the baby away.

"Good idea." Haldane turned and went to see how the nurse was doing.

A Creon doctor in a smock was hovering over her, clucking concernedly.

"How's she doing, Doc?"

The doctor wagged his eyebrows at him. "She'll be fine, but I want to put her into detoxification at the local hospital."

"What! Who's going to look after the kid then?"

"That will be your job."

"Job, shmob. It's bad enough being responsible for the little monster's safety. Dealing with him moment to moment—no . . ." He turned to a security officer. "Get me Central."

"I believe it's necessary to make the phone call yourself," said the guard.

"Then get me a remote comm!"

"That I can do."

The guard pulled one off his belt. Within moments, Haldane was in contact with Took.

"Tookie, we've had a little trouble here," he said, and explained the situation. "I was hoping you could get the next shift nurse to come in a little bit earlier than planned."

There was no response. "I'm sorry, is there something wrong with the line? I'm not getting anything from you."

"No. It's just that I was about to call you, Jack."

"Oh?"

"Yes. The next qualified shift nurse has emergency all-night telekinetic surgery. There's absolutely no one I can replace her with."

"What?"

"I was rather hoping that you and Jane could tuck the little tyke in tonight."

"WHAT!"

"It's not that hard. Look, I'll be in myself and help change diapers or whatever. . . ."

"Tookie . . . Can't you hear what I've been saying to you? This child is a MENACE!"

"All the better to have a pair of qualified police officer to deal with him, Jack."

"Not *this* police officer."

"Pardon?" Took was cool.

"I didn't come light-years across space to . . . to . . . to babysit Godzilla Junior."

"Oh. I see. Racial slurs along with your insubordination," said Took.

"Since when are you my superior?"

"Look, if you'd like, I can call Podly up right now and settle this entire matter once and for all."

That gave Jack Haldane pause. He visualized Podly's big overbearing face jammed into his, his deep voice giving him absolute hell.

And he'd be saying the exact same thing as Took was saying now. No question.

Haldane sighed. "And I suppose I'm the one who has to give Jane these wonderful tidings."

"If I may observe, Jack . . . I believe I see maternal aspects in our Officer Castle. She may feel ill at ease but perhaps secretly she will *enjoy* this challenge." There was a reflective pause. "Besides, in your biological makeup, is not reproduction the logical consequence, indeed the *reason* for sexual congress. . . ."

"Well yeah . . ."

"And if you successfully temporarily parent Yanx with Jane, will she not see you as a more likely partner and therefore instinctively want to mate with you? And isn't mating the goal you seek in your relationship with Jane?"

"Well, now that you're spelling it out in graphic sociobiological terms . . . I'm rather put off."

"In that case, just look at the whole matter as your civic duty, Jack. Well, there's no more time to talk about it. I'll be checking in with you later, as promised. Goodbye."

Before Haldane could say anything, she had disconnected.

They were stuck with the kid.

Oh well, thought Haldane. How bad could it be?

And then he realized: With this kid, pretty bad. He'd better go out and give Jane the news. . . .

And then it struck him: she'd taken Yanx out to where they'd been playing that game.

Out with the cards!

He hustled through the room. When he entered the game room, he immediately saw Jane holding and coddling Yanx, the cards within easy telekinetic reach of that mischievous and powerful young mind.

"Jane, no—" He said, hurrying over.

"Jack, what's wrong—?"

He increased his speed. All he had to do was reach the cards, put his hands on them so they wouldn't float up, destroying their order—and his winning hand . . .

That's all—

However, between him and his goal was an unruly bit of rug that made acquaintance with his shoe.

He tripped, arms flapping desperately. . . .

. . . And came down right on top of the game of gin, hopelessly scattering the cards.

"Jack! You did that on purpose! You *knew* I had the winning hand, didn't you?" said Jane. "How unsportsmanlike!"

Yanx started laughing. "Splat!"

Jack looked up mournfully at them both staring down at him. "Couldn't have said it better myself," he sighed.

CHAPTER 15

When Patrick Brogan was a student at the Police Academy, he had been taught the various ways of disarming a person headed his way wielding a knife. They all had a great deal to do with such martial arts as judo and involved using the individual's momentum and energy in one's own favor.

However, in the street, if a person came one's way with a knife, the general wisdom was that the necessary procedure was drawing out one's gun and wasting said assailant.

Thus was Brogan's first impulse when that monk started wailing and running their way with an upraised knife was to pull his gun and waste the guy. In fact, Officer Fleur did the exact same thing.

However, he realized that dead Creons told no tales, and they'd come there that day not for gun battles but for information.

"Wait," he said. "Don't shoot him."

He flipped the gun around and used the broad side as a shield. He put himself in front of the hooded Creon's charge, feinted. The wailing man lunged at him, knifepoint first. Brogan dodged. With his free hand, he grabbed his assailant's wrist. As he'd been taught in self-defense class, he used the attacker's momentum against the attacker.

Alas, the attacker's angle and size played against the possibility of his getting flipped and easily put out of commission. Instead of flipping, Brogan whipped the man past him against a wall.

The knife clattered harmlessly to the floor.

Brogan paused a moment to assay the situation.

It was a moment too long.

As soon as the Creon hit the wall, he bounced off and was immediately running away, with surprising speed for someone of his bulk and size.

At the near end of the room was a flight of stairs. The Creon disappeared up them, his robe flapping in his wake.

"After him!" called Brogan.

Officer Fleur was closest, and she responded immediately, ripping across the room and tearing up the steps, pistol stiff in its regulation position, cocked above her shoulder by her ear.

"Halt!" she cried.

Brogan was on her heels.

They sprinted up the dark, narrow, fusty steps. The stairs were a little damp and thus Brogan found himself losing his footing, but he managed to keep himself upright.

The stairs went up and up, finally ending in an open chamber filled with old urns and boxes. Brogan could hear the fugitive bumping and clattering through this obstacle course, with Christina still calling to him from behind.

A sudden wash of light.

A door had been opened.

As he quickly picked his way over the boxes and bumps in the storage attic, Brogan heard the Creon lumbering out onto the rooftops. Then came Officer Fleur's lighter steps.

"Stop or I'll shoot!"

He hoped she didn't mean it.

He tripped once, twice, and got a faceful of a dust cloud kicked up by the pursued and first pursuer.

Then he broke out into the sunlight.

He had to squint at first until his eyes adjusted. But he kept moving as well as he could, following the forms that bounced and jerked in front of him.

They came into focus.

The buildingscape of this part of Demeter City was like something out of Victorian London, only half-melted. Some of it didn't even looked solid, but somehow the previously meditating monk found footing as he hurried away at a surprising speed for someone so large and bulky.

Christina was not far behind. She'd given up on her gun and now looked as though she were just trying to get close enough to tackle the guy.

Brogan hurried after them, looking for an opportunity to take a shortcut and head the Creon off.

The pursued started zigzagging. He reached a crest, and Brogan saw his chance.

He could hurry around a chimneylike protuberance, attain a higher position, and then jump down on his quarry.

Puffing, he hurried up the incline.

At the top, he looked down.

There was the Creon, with Christina right behind.

Brogan prepared to jump.

Suddenly, though, there was a loud report. The Creon arched backward, grabbed at his back as though to pull something out—

And then fell.

"Christina!" called Brogan.

"I didn't shoot him!" returned his partner.

Brogan jumped down from the rise, pushed Christina out of the way.

The Creon was writhing on the ground, mouth opening and closing as though trying to say something.

Finally, words gasped out.

"You have summoned the God of Evil, and destroyed this world. Let the payment of destiny weigh heavy upon all our heads."

"Who has summoned the God?" said Brogan.

"The Unrevered Ones from Afar." Blood bubbled from his mouth. "Our Church has been a pawn. A pawn to this rankest of unholiness . . ."

The last words were just sputters and gurgles.

The big head tilted suddenly.

Dead.

"He's gone," said Brogan.

"Yes, and we can thank our Patron Saint here," said Christina. Her gun was out and she was looking back toward the exit from which they'd emerged. Her gun was poised and ready to fire in that direction.

Standing there, holding a smoking device that looked like a cross between a rifle and a crossbow, adorned with brass protuberances and odd gagas, was Kawkor.

"He rests now, dangerous to no one," intoned the Ardentian priest.

"We had the situation under control, dammit," said Brogan. He held up his own gun. "Now why don't you put that weapon down and tell us exactly what is going on?"

Sausage-face obeyed, placing the device he'd killed the monk with on the rooftop.

"Now hold your arms up in the air," ordered Christina.

"My joints will not allow such a position," objected the priest.

"Then just stick your limbs out of your robes."

Seven appendages of various lengths suddenly slid through slits in his robe.

"Is that all of them?" demanded Christina.

"Quiet or he might show his reproductive limb," said Brogan, grimacing.

"How do we know one of those things isn't it?"

"Let's not ask." However, Brogan knew what question was necessary to ask of the priest. "Did you hear what your acolyte said with his dying breaths?"

"My hearing is not that acute, Officer Brogan."

Brogan repeated the words verbatim.

The priest's robes rippled. Brogan assumed that it was his species form of a shrug.

"I do not know what that means. We are a peaceful group. We merely perform our arcane and ancient rituals, meditate and hope that the energies of our reflections generate peace and good will throughout the Universe."

Yeah. Right, thought Brogan.

And the pope golfed on the moon.

"I'm going to have to request that you show us around your rooms and explain a little more to us," said Brogan.

"Alas, that will not be possible," said the priest, his limbs and face-sausage wriggling in an upset manner worthy of a sea anemone in a rough current. "There are areas of our chambers that are highly sacred, and only anointed feet may tread there with safety and sanctity."

"Well, you'd better get your anointers out then, buddy," said Brogan, hoisting his gun higher. "'Cos these feet are going to be traveling soon."

"These kinds of tactics are not advisable," said the priest. "This is police intimidation. The laws I know are not merely celestial ones."

Brogan lowered his gun and nodded to Christina. "He's right. We're going to have to get a search warrant."

"Is that possible?"

"Oh yes. Particularly in light of the dear departed." He nodded down to the dead Creon. "We just have to do a little bit of paperwork back at the office, that's all. Once this has all been cleaned up, of course."

The priest merely stood there, wriggling quietly to himself.

Podly threw the paper down on the desk.

"Here it is," he boomed grumpily. "I had to pull teeth and a few unmentionable body parts to ram this through. But you now have permission to do a thorough search of that temple. Question is, I'm still not certain what you think you're going to find."

This bureaucratic process had taken hours, and Brogan had the sick feeling that whatever would do them any good back at the temple would have long since been hidden by now. On the other hand, the other cops who had been summoned to deal with the problem had set up a cordon around the area.

No one was going to leave the temple without their knowing about it.

"I've got a gut feeling that we'll find what we're looking for in there," said Brogan. "What that monk said seems to indicate that there's some kind of link between the cult and the creature. . . . And we've got the death of that businessman as the vital link. . . . The rest just call gut instinct."

Podly nodded. "You're a good cop, Brogan. You've got a good gut. A pretty lean one, true, but a good one." Podly smiled grimly. "That's why I'm going with you on this thing."

"Thanks, Captain. I appreciate that."

"Officer Fleur. This is quite a lot we're asking you on your first day on the job. Are you sure you're up to it?" said Podly, his face softening somewhat.

"Absolutely certain, sir," said the woman. "I can see that Lieutenant Brogan is a fine policeman. I couldn't wish to work with anyone better."

"And for my part I should say that Officer Fleur performed quite well on our first day together," said Brogan.

Podly grunted. "Good. Then you'll have some overtime tonight together."

That was fine by Brogan. Besides, he'd already talked to his wife. She was all for getting to the bottom of this matter. Moreover, she said she was doing some kind of volunteer work tonight, anyway.

"So what are you standing there looking at my beautiful mug for?" said Podly. "Go check that place out!"

Brogan took the search warrant and stuck it in his pocket.

"Yes sir!"

The two cops turned and went back to work in Demeter City.

CHAPTER 16

Feeding a baby was bad enough.

The prospect of feeding a telekinetic baby was quite another thing altogether.

Or so, at least, Haldane thought, as the dreaded hour approached.

However, as dinner drew near, although Yanx did not seem to become tired (apparently Tarn babies did not have a pressing need for naps, alas), he did not seem the happy and gay creature that he'd been all afternoon. Haldane almost wished he would float a pet or two, just for old times' sake.

"He's sad," said Castle, looking analytically at Yanx, as he sat on the couch, head propped forlornly on a pillow.

"Sad? Why?"

"I suspect he's beginning to miss his parents," said Jane, peering down sympathetically at their small charge. "Do you miss your mommy and daddy, poor Yanxie?"

Yanx said nothing, merely staring off into space as though the weight of the world was on those tiny shoulders.

"Hmmm. Could be. He does seem a touch forlorn. A bit more mature than before, as well. A little melancholy isn't such a bad thing, it would seem."

The tyke sighed, looked up at him as though his heart would break, then his chin drooped to his chest.

Jack Haldane experienced an unpleasant sensation in the region of his own chest.

Indigestion?

No, dammit.

The little bastard was tugging at his heart.

Sheesh! What the hell was he coming to?

"Maybe he'll feel better after dinner." He bent over and tickled the Tarn child. "Hey there. How 'bout a little dinnie-poo, soldier?"

Yanx just shrugged and resumed his black funk.

"Dinnie-poo?" said Jane, hands on her hips.

"Isn't that what Tarns call it?"

"No, I don't think so. In any event, we've got lots of it. Fortunately for us, the nurse made plenty before she met with her unfortunate accident. I just had to heat it up."

Jack's stomach rumbled.

"Say, I'm a little peckish myself. What's for us?"

"I do believe that some beans and franks have been shipped in for you. And a balanced vegetarian and bulgur wheat meal has been sent for me."

"Vulgar wheat? I'm looking forward to seeing that."

"If you'll just step this way, the dinner table is set. And if you'd be so good, please bring our little friend."

"Sure. C'mon, champ."

Jack picked Yanx up. The baby felt like deadweight, not responding at all. Jack quickly made sure there was a pulse. There wasn't, but the baby did eye him suspiciously.

"C'mon. Let's go eat."

He brought the baby out to the kitchen area, where Jane had set the table.

"Right here on the high chair," directed Jane.

Jack set Yanx down. The baby made no objection.

"I'll just go and get a bowl of his dinner."

"Mmmm. What do we have here?" said Jack, picking up a lid from the turreen nearest him. In the dish was a delightful brown concoction of beans and franks. It smelled absolutely delicious, speaking savory notes of ketchup and more ketchup in the sauce.

"Yum."

"Yum," said Yanx, suddenly enthusiastic.

"I'd give you some, but I'm not sure it would be right for you!"

"Yum!" The baby reached for the dish.

Jack looked up, calculating. It did give him a good feeling to see Yanx smiling again. "Well, okay. But eat it quickly before Aunt Jane comes back."

He put some in a spoon and handed it to Yanx, who swallowed it all in a quick gulp.

"Yum!" said the baby, reaching out for more.

"Well well. Sure. I guess if it wasn't fit for your

system you wouldn't like it. Just one more, though." Jack gave him another spoonful, which Yanx ate with equal enthusiasm.

Jack pulled the spoon back just in time before Jane Castle came in.

"Well, this is what was in the pot, so I assume that it's what Tarn babies like."

Jack smiled to himself. *He* knew now what Tarn babies liked.

However, when he looked down at Yanx, he saw that the child had a bemused look on his face. Like he was trying to figure out some kind of complex mathematical equation.

"Here you go, dear," said Jane, putting the bowl of whatever it was before the baby.

Yanx just stared at it.

"What is that, exactly?"

"I haven't the faintest."

"It smells . . ." Jack's lip tilted at one end. "Well, not exactly appetizing."

"Let's not be culturally narrow," said Jane. "I'm sure it's wholesome and exactly the sort of thing that Tarn babies need to grow healthy and strong. Right, darling."

Yanx's lips curled as he looked down at the bowl of gruelish-looking material.

"Yuck," said Yanx.

"Ah. A new word added to a wide vocabulary," said Jack. "How special."

"I'd imagine he got it from the author of 'vulgar wheat'," said Jane. She turned to Yanx. "Now be a good boy and eat your dinner."

"Yuck!" said Yanx, louder and more emphatically, as though he was uncertain if she had heard him before. He pushed the dish away.

"Maybe if you ate some yourself, he'd see that it's not only delicious . . . but that it won't kill him," said Jack.

Jane seemed skeptical.

"Oh, come on."

"I'm not sure what it is. I mean, it could be, oh dear—unimaginable things. Squiggly things from the bottoms of alien seas . . . rotting plants from some sunless jungle . . ." A truly horrified look appeared on her face. "Maybe even . . . dare I utter the words . . . hot dogs!"

"Hey. Nothing wrong with hot dogs."

She took her fork and made a tentative stab at the gruel.

"There you go. He seems interested now."

Indeed, Jack Haldane's observation was true. Yanx seemed very intent upon observing the result of Jane's taste test.

"Well . . . very well."

Carefully, Jane scooped out some of the stuff, brought it to her mouth. She delicately placed the fork inside her mouth . . .

. . . then swiftly brought it out again.

"Oh dear," she said.

Yanx started giggling and generally having a high old time.

"You see. You don't expect this kid to eat *that,* do you?"

"I really think I ought to go and consult a higher

authority on this matter," said Jane. "I'll just use the comm in the next room."

"You do that. Yanx and I will stay here and have a man-to-man talk."

Jane left, and Haldane swung his attention back to the baby. Was that his imagination or was Yanx *floating* perhaps a half inch off his high chair?

Naw.

If the kid had been unhappy before, those blues had been banished. He was all smiles.

"Yeah. That was pretty funny, wasn't it?"

"Blatt!" The kid was pointing at his beans and franks again.

"I don't think I'd better let you have any more, Yanx."

"Splat!"

"Is that a threat?"

The head turned inquisitively, then shook.

"Hey. Maybe you're beginning to understand me. Look, guy . . . there's got to be some kind of treat you're allowed. I'll just go in and see if I can yank the information from the experts."

When he walked into the next room, Jane was on the phone. When she saw him, her reaction was immediate. "What are you doing here? You're supposed to be watching Yanx."

"I think the kid deserves some kind of treat. Ask about a treat for him, will you?"

"Yes, yes . . . Now get back in there."

"He's trying to communicate!"

"Haldane! Get your fat head—No, Took, I didn't

call you a fathead. I was speaking to Haldane. Yes . . . it is rather large, isn't it?"

Feeling his face self-consciously, Jack Haldane walked back into the dining area. Hmm. Maybe he *was* eating too many hot dogs . . . He knew he should watch his svelte figure, but he'd never considered his face . . .

Maybe low-fat ketchup in the future would do the trick.

Maybe . . .

As he entered the room, he immediately saw that things were not as they should be. Fortunately, Yanx was still in his high chair. Unfortunately, the dish of beans and franks had somehow gotten on Yanx's tray and he was busy wolfing the stuff down. . . .

"Yanx!"

"Yum!" said Yanx.

Jack was so stunned that the baby had time to cram two entire handfuls into his maw. With a pained expression, Jack yanked the dish away from the Tarn baby.

A surprised expression came onto the baby's face.

He blinked and seemed to be in the middle of deciding what attitude to take next.

Then he started wailing.

Hmmm. *Too* much like a human baby for Jack's taste.

"Yanx! Hey . . . I didn't eat those beans and franks. *You* ate the beans and franks. In fact, because of you"—and here, Jack pointed meaningfully at the

Tarn child—"I don't get to eat my beans and franks."

The baby paused nary a second in its neo-existential wailing. Indeed, if anything, the sound increased in volume.

Jane entered. "Jack. Whatever is going on in—" Stopped in astonishment. "Jack. You let the baby eat the beans and franks."

"He *likes* beans and franks."

"But it's not Tarn food."

"Look, it's organic. It's biodegradable. . . . And not only that, it's wholesome and American. What more could you possibly want out of food?"

Suddenly, all of the dishes and plates and glasses began rising into the air.

Last of all went Yanx, who had stopped crying now, and was merely looking stunned and disoriented again.

"Grab him, Jack."

Jack, a former wide receiver in college football, snapped to attention. Almost before he knew it, he leaped up . . . and caught Yanx by the ankle.

His weight immediately brought the baby down and Jack immediately got a more secure hold on him.

"It would seem that human food—beans and franks at least—does indeed have a negative effect on Tarn babies."

The tableware crashed down with messy results.

"How do you know it was the beans and franks?" sked Jack. "It could be anything."

Yanx chose that unfortunate moment to cough,

then suddenly to projectile-vomit the conspicuously brown contents of his stomach down the front of Jack's shirt.

"Out of the mouths of babes," said Jane, arms folded in her damnably unsexy I-told-you-so stance.

Yanx hiccuped and smiled.

Standing there, dripping, in the center of this huge mess, his erstwhile hope for romance staring at him as though he were lowlier than the upchuck that decorated him, Jack Haldane wondered, *How can things possibly get worse?*

That was when the lights went out.

CHAPTER 17

The politician took Sally Brogan's hand and practically swallowed it with a damp, unpleasant kiss.

"I'm so happy you could make it this evening," said the unctuous host and guest speaker, Joseph Salamander, all smiles as he took a moment to personally welcome each of the volunteers for their special Earther meeting.

His welcome was a bit *too* personal for Sally Brogan's taste, and his slimy lips lingered a bit too long. He kissed the way she fancied a Republican smooched his money.

It gave her the creeps.

Nonetheless, that was why she was here, right. She had the feeling this conservative Earth politician was . . . well, a phony Earth conservative politician.

Not that she and her husband didn't have *some* conservative traits. But then, Sally had pretty much come to the conclusion that a middle-of-the-road attitude was the most workable. The problem with ultraliberals and ultraconservatives was pretty much the same: intolerance of other philosophies. Sally Brogan's sympathies were primarily liberal for a simple reason. A conservative mind-set saw the human soul as a static, base commodity, redeemable only by God or money. A liberal attitude accepted problems, but believed in working toward a better future. The human spirit was something that was in the midst of a wonderful adventure: evolution. Not merely biologically evolving, but multidimensionally evolving.

Everything she had encountered in this brave new Universe showed her this was true. All the wonderful varieties of life, philosophies, imaginations, spiritualities, joys, and characters . . . when you had the right attitude (and the intelligence to deal with the differences) you could conquer everything. . . .

Eventually.

But the right attitude was of paramount importance.

And something told her that this glibly smiling good ol' boy from Men's Club, Earth, was packing some seriously Bad Attitude that would do the human presence in Demeter City . . . indeed, the human presence in the Universe itself . . . absolutely no good.

Which was why she was here: to check this Salamander guy out a little more closely.

"Thanks so much," she said to the politician, turning the wattage of her smile up a little higher.

"I truly enjoyed your talk the other day. There are problems here. I'd like to get involved with any movement that will help make the Universe safer for my children."

Good. Just enough baloney to give her sincerity sandwich some meat.

A bushy eyebrow rose. The eye below it appraised her. She could see he was having possibility-thoughts about her. It gave her the willies, but she managed to keep her smile in place.

"Excellent. Well, then, you must excuse me, but I must go and welcome the newcomers. But perhaps we might get together for coffee later . . ."

Uh-oh.

She got a definite whiff of predatory sexual interest. What was this jerk thinking? He knew she was married . . .

But then, of course, power tended to bend moral rules around such things as personal conquest.

"Well, tonight's not good, I'm afraid, but perhaps later in your stay."

Another member of the group achieved the politician's attention by touching his elbow, and the man had to be on his way, but not before a lecherous twinkle toward Sally glimmered in the man's eye.

Ugh.

She got a cup of coffee and took her place in the circle of seats, trying to keep to herself and hoping that no one there recognized her. She certainly didn't recognize anyone, and that was just fine. Not that she couldn't eventually explain why she was here. It would simply make things complicated.

Finally, half a cup of coffee later, the meeting got under way.

Salamander briefly thanked them for coming, standing before them in a particularly friendly and avuncular manner.

"I'm glad that all of you care enough for the status of Earth—and humanity—in the cosmos to take the time to volunteer to carry the lights of our hearts and hopes.

"At this moment, two significant things are occurring. A form is being passed out, and we're merely asking you fill in the information requested, including the spare hours you might be able to use to canvass your human friends, neighbors, and strangers about our cause.

"The other thing occurring is the passing out of a packet that includes literature and information concerning our cause. These are for you to peruse at your leisure . . . but we'd encourage you to get right down to that task, because it will facilitate the communication of our ideas and concepts to other humans here on Demeter City . . . and the other parts of the Universe to which humanity is spreading."

He took a dramatic pause, and his dark piercing eyes gazed out at his audience. Those agate orbs seemed to focus on each of the fifteen-odd humans there, registering upon them individually the seriousness of what was transpiring.

When they settled on Sally, she felt as though they were peering deeply into her, through her, picking out all her secret thoughts . . .

But then, they moved on to her neighbor, a man in a gray business suit and loosened tie. . . .

And those eyes bored into his with equal intensity and force.

A trick. A speaker's trick to indicate sincerity and meaningfulness. Who knew . . . maybe ol' Salamander had even rigged himself up with a Harmonic Emitter, to vibrate properly with the audience. . . . There'd always been things leaders knew about making people listen to them. With the scientific revolutions of the past century, it had merely become easier for the unaware and unsuspecting to get wrapped up in the snares of the kind of grandiloquence Salamander clearly radiated.

"You've proved to me that we have similar thought processes by being here tonight. I feel I have a friendlier audience, so I'll let you know a little more of what I'm about, and hope that this will cause yet more of an affiliation between us."

He sat down in a chair as though to show that he was, indeed, one of them. His voice grew less stentorian and formal, and it became more of a fireside-chat kind of affair.

"I'm a little bit higher up in government than you are, folks," he said.

Polite laughter.

"There are things I know that you might not necessarily be aware of that have been happening on very high levels. Knowledge filtering in." He picked up a spare packet, slapped it. "Much of it is in here, but I'll do you the favor of giving you the basic summary:

"Mankind is in trouble in this new Universe.

"We are in trouble on many fronts . . . one, of course, being Democrats . . ." Smile.

Honest chuckles.

"Just kidding, folks. I don't see anything about Democrats that a little stark reality can't cure. When humanity's back is against the wall, it will be white backs, black backs, and backs of all political persuasions.

"No, the threat in fact is outside of Earth. . . .

"We have come too far too fast, and there are races of aliens who would have us on our knees. They pretend they are allowing us to integrate among the stars while they seek to separate us from what is most valuable to us—our heritage and our destiny.

"I feel I can trust you all. So now I will tell you what troubles me the most.

"I have evidence that the various alien races who have representatives among us on Earth are all in conspiracy not merely to take our planet away from us"—he let the 's' stretch out to great a hissing sibilance—"but to sully our very DNA!"

That announcement lingered in the air like a sudden blast of bad air. The members of the group looked as though they were riveted and fascinated.

It was all that Sally could do to prevent herself from standing up and debating with the man. She'd realized that he was carrying trouble and turmoil with him, but nothing to this extent.

Sally had read that there were Earth First groups back home, and people who believed that mankind should not traffic with alien races as equals. She'd always classified them with Flat Earthers and Luddites. She never thought it would be possible for such narrow minds to be able to rise to political power. . . .

But then, that was ever the failing of those who took the advancement of general human attitudes for granted. . . .

"Wait a minute. What are you suggesting?" said a man. "That we should withdraw from the stars, go back home, and build force fields or something? Strikes me that things have gone a little too far for that."

Salamander nodded soberly. "Yes. Indeed they have. No, I think that mankind cannot retreat." His voice grew steely and hard. "However, we must be aware of the situation we are in now. And we must be prepared to act. . . . Prepared to take our rightful place among the stars. . . . Prepared to carry out our destiny . . . particularly at this vital crossroads.

"This is a dangerous place, fraught with peril. We must heed the messages the Universe gives us. We must take matters in our own hands . . . and rally . . ."

He smiled sadly.

"But then, I'm sure you are all aware of this. Subliminally, if nothing more."

Again, the sincere and probing stare.

"If I were a more proselytzingly religious man—" He caught himself. "No, I won't get into that. Let's just say, look for signs."

He went on for a while in this same vein, and

then began feverishly talking about the "Green Hills of Earth" and the pride which one inherited, being a homo sapiens.

There was no doubt about it: the man was a raging homeocentric. But then, this was not uncommon among the stars, thought Sally. Was it indeed true that 'Man is the measure of all things'? What other attitude could the rationalists of prespace settlement take? Adjustment out in the Universe was indeed difficult. You had to know and love your own species before you could hope to understand other species. . . .

On the other hand, this kind of poison was absolute anathema to the possibility of the dream of peace among the planets. The man never actually said it, but he veered terribly close to positing a notion of an "Earthman's Burden." Within the parameters of what he was saying, it would be easy to imagine the next logical steps that this organization would suggest: segregation of species, studies of weapons systems, and, finally, a kind of OverPolice action on the part of mankind, once they came up to speed scientifically and technologically.

In short, subjugation of the stars.

Oh, Salamander didn't actually *say* this. However, Sally could read it all between the lines.

And it appalled her.

What appalled her even more was the way the group was eating it up. Sally could understand how one could feel homesick and alienated here on Demeter City. Naturally it was an instinctive thing to want to be with your own kind. However, she'd always hoped that whoever had the bravery to come out here would also realize, as she did, that it would take some sacrifices and some effort to work with other intelligent beings. You had to put the emphasis on similarities and common goals rather than differences. Couldn't they see that this was the lesson that history taught humanity from its trials among its own peoples?

This was even worse than she thought.

Sally also had the profound feeling that if this man were capable of these divisive and damaging announcements in public—then what he must be trying to accomplish behind the scenes on Demeter would be just as deadly.

Sally shivered with the thought.

However, she knew that she was going to have to find out what she could.

Salamander finished up with a few quotes from famous people—fantastically skewed, Sally noticed—and then promised that his principal people would be in contact with everyone who filled out a form.

There were coffee and snacks afterward, and Salamander spent time with each of the group, all of whom seemed very caught up in his charisma.

"Mrs. Brogan," beamed the politician. "Now can we make a date for that coffee? I can sense that you're just the kind of person I need for an important position."

Yeah, right, thought Sally. *The missionary position.*

"Of course. However, lunch would work much better for me! I know a terrific place. Private but pleasant."

Salamander's eyes lit up. "Lunch! But of course! A splendid idea. Would one o'clock suit you?"

"Perfectly."

"Only I hope that this is a human-run establishment. I confess I'm not very comfortable being around aliens when I eat."

"Yes. It's a little café that makes hamburgers and french fries by the Earth Embassy. It's called Wimpy's Dream and I'll write down the address for you."

"Excellent. I'll look forward to it then."

She found a piece of paper and a pen and wrote down the information. He thanked her and then went on to talk to other people. While she was sipping her coffee and absently talking to another woman, she eyed the area.

It didn't take her long to find what she was looking for: the women's room. After a few more minutes, as people were slowly filing out, she excused herself from her conversation and made her way to a room in a small alcove, tucked away in the back behind a partition. She tried to walk as discreetly and as quietly as possible, so as to call no notice to herself. As she walked, she paid attention peripherally to the stragglers in the meeting room.

As best she could tell, no one noticed where she was going.

When she got into the bathroom, she went to the stall especially fitted for humans, put down the seat of a commode, pulled up her legs, and settled in for a wait.

She let five minutes go by.

Ten.

She'd better go check now, she thought. Swung her legs down. Quietly walked to the door.

Peeked out.

She saw nothing. And, at first, heard nothing. Then, she made out the sound of a man talking in the distance. Talking, pausing. Talking. A man on a comm unit of some sort.

However, she couldn't make out what he was saying. She had to venture out a little farther. Besides, then she could match visual with auditory.

Quietly as she could, she ventured out, closing the door behind her silently, walking to the edge of the partition, peering out cautiously.

There, at the far end of the room, was Salamander. He was alone, with his back to her, and she could see the telltale narrow portable comm tube.

". . . I see . . ." said Salamander. "I see . . ."

Hmm. Not a whole lot of information there. She bided her time, though.

"Well, I'm very sorry to hear that. There's nothing you can do to stall or even prevent the investigation? Yes, I understand, there's only so much you can do. I'm just happy that you're there, period. You're in the exact spot that we need you right now. What? Yes, you heard me correctly. From everything we can tell, the creature will be attacking again tonight. . . . Yes, at exactly the proper time to make maximum media exposure. . . . Yes, yes . . . that's fine. . . . The important thing is that you make sure that there is *no* evidence, *no* link between that bizarre killing alien and me or my organization . . . yes. . . . That's fine. . . . That's absolutely excellent. . . . You see, there's a plus in our scorecard if humans are killed. . . . Particularly if they're cops. . . . We'll have both humanity and the police on our side . . ."

There was a pause.

Salamander spoke again, only this time too faintly to be heard.

This was vital information. Sally stepped out a little farther. Still she couldn't hear. She stepped around to a chair.

Suddenly, Salamander turned around.

Sally ducked behind the chair.

It really was inadequate covering, but it was the best she could do, given the situation. Fortunately Salamander didn't seem to notice her. He kept right on talking.

"Yes. Yes. . . ."

His eyes looked over toward her, but off into the less shadowed areas. He had none of the appealing coloring or expressions while in a social situation.

He looked just as amphibious as his name.

"Brogan?" said Salamander. "Yes, there's the little matter of Patrick Brogan, isn't there?"

Pause.

Patrick?

Sally felt her heart rushing into her throat.

"If Brogan is a problem," continued Salamander, "then kill him. But be sure it looks as though it was done by an alien. They're the villains, here. . . . And they truly are . . . Never, ever forget that . . . and never forget the noble cause that we stand for—the fulfillment of mankind's destiny in the Universe. . . ."

Sally couldn't believe her ears. This politician was ordering someone to kill her husband. And it all had something to do with this whole incredible Earth First business.

She had to get in contact with Patrick!

Alas, she'd brought no comm unit with her. She was stuck here in the back of this room.

She'd have to wait to get out until Salamander left.

But when would that be? Would it be in time?

Salamander turned around again.

Sally took the opportunity to immediately hurry back to the partition, diving behind it, tucking her feet in as quickly as possible.

She paused a breathless moment, listening.

At first she heard nothing. She thought, *He's heard me! He and his deadly right-wing paramilitary monsters, equipped with their array of huge weapons, will be on me any moment now and I'll never see my children again!*

Fortunately, nothing of the kind happened.

Eventually Salamander's voice filtered through again: "That's right. That's right. Good. Okay. . . . Yes, I'll see you soon. Good-bye."

He was silent.

Sally heard the sound of retreating footsteps, and then the sound of a door slamming.

Whew!

She let out a breath, and gave herself a little time to pause and reflect and collect herself before venturing back out into the room.

Patrick, in danger.

The whole plan for Earth to venture peacefully out among the stars was in jeopardy!

She had to go and call Patrick, call *all* the authorities as soon as possible.

As soon as she felt it was safe, she tiptoed back out into the room. It was dark, but still she could navigate her way, if she was careful.

Slowly, carefully, she went to the door.

Quietly, she put her hand on the knob.

Twisted.

Panic threatened to overcome her.

The door was locked!

She was stuck inside this room!

CHAPTER 13

The temple—indeed, the whole area of town surrounding it—exhibited a distinct difference at night.

It wasn't just the grimness, the odd shadows, and the way that the lights looked like the eyes of nasty demons staring out at them from the walls. Nor was it simply the way the air and atmosphere had a particularly noxious aspect to them, thought Patrick Brogan as he opened the door of the police cruiser and stepped onto the cobblestone surface of the alleyway beside the oozing building.

It was the *feel* of the place.

"Cripes," he said. "It *feels* evil," he said to Officer Christina Fleur as she stepped over beside him and they stood, regarding the place.

"Well, it's darker, that's for certain."

"Gives me the creeps. I think I'll call for backup."

"That would be smart," said the woman. "I was wondering why you weren't doing it before."

"To be honest, I didn't see it as that much of a problem," said Brogan. "I figured we two could handle it if we worked together. Besides, we're shorthanded, what with all the forces we have detailed watching that kid and at other places in the city."

"That's true."

"No, though, now that I get a look at this place . . ."

"Say no more. I know what you mean."

He went to the radio, punched it on.

Nothing happened.

"I can't get anything. What's happening with your mobile?" said Brogan.

Christina pulled out her comm. Touched a button.

"Funny. Just static."

He pulled out his.

Static.

"Damn. Same thing."

"You want to go back?"

Brogan thought about it for a moment. "No. Chances are we can't get any more men, anyway."

"There's no guarantee we're going to find anything here, anyway," Christina said.

Brogan looked at the place.

"True. Just because there's something there they don't want us to see doesn't mean it's dangerous or something that has to do with this creature . . ." She unbuttoned the holster of her gun. "On the other hand, I don't know about you, but I'm ready for just about anything."

Brogan nodded.

His holster was already unbuttoned.

"Okay. Then I guess all that remains is to show them this." He pulled out their search warrant.

"I checked. By all accounts, this particular religion seems particularly law-abiding."

He rattled the paper. "Well, we've got the law here." Brogan nodded toward the door. "Let's go use it."

Their progress was a repeat of earlier, only lit by the feeble quivers of very questionable street lighting, along with a billowing moon just lifting up over the ragged skyline. Approaching, there was a particularly fetid smell in the air, as though garbage collectors not only didn't pick up here, they delivered.

They knocked on the door.

It opened.

Kawkor, the same monk as before, answered. Sausage-face. Looking particularly meaty tonight.

"Greetings and good evening."

Brogan began to hold up the paper.

"No need, officers. We've been expecting you." The monk stepped aside, gestured them in. "Come this way."

Brogan and Christina exchanged glances.

"We're expecting to see everything we want to."

"Of course. That is why you have brought the search warrant, no?"

Brogan thought a moment.

They'd put a spotter on this place, and there was absolutely no recorded movement in or out of the place. What was going on?

If they had nothing to hide, why had they not shown them everything before?

The notion of underground activity crossed his mind.

However, he'd brought a sensor unit with him. If there were underground passageways, he'd find them.

Again they reached the central chamber. However, this time there were no meditating monks, nor any other sign of life.

"Where are the other inhabitants?" said Brogan.

"We are early risers," explained Kawkor. "They have all retired for the evening."

"We'd like to verify that."

"Of course. I'll be happy to take you to the resting pools when you are finished with your search."

Resting pools?

The image was not the most pleasant that Brogan could conjure up.

"Where would you like to look first?" asked Kawkor, almost unctuously.

"I don't understand," said Christina. "Your cooperation was extremely limited this morning. Why the sudden change of heart now?"

"Heart?" said the alien monk. "Oh! Pulmonary pump. That's correct, it is associated with a center of feelings in the human race. How very curious. What you mean, then, is 'change of attitude,' perhaps?"

"Look, I don't mean to be a bossy, nasty cop—but we've got a job to do. Could we get on with it?"

"Ah, yes. Well. If you're concerned about wasting

your time—there is an area that I did not show you before that you'll want to see now."

Brogan cocked his head. "I don't understand. What is it?"

He could feel his hand twitching toward his gun. He felt suddenly nervous and suspicious.

"It is possibly something that might be of help to you in your investigation," said the monk, robes billowing as he beckoned them onward. "The reason I could not show it to you was that it was day. We monks are constrained by the presence of the rays of the sun upon Demeter City. Now that the sun is gone, we are less bonded with it, and can help you."

"You're saying you're implicated?" said Christina.

"I said no such thing," replied the monk. "What you are about to see might perhaps be considered a divining system that can be of help in what you seek. It is strictly forbidden that it be revealed in the daylight hours. However, now I am happy to be of whatever help I can."

Brogan exchanged doubtful and wondering looks with Officer Christina Fleur.

They were led down a dank corridor to a large door, composed of some kind of fibrous oak.

The robed monk took out a dangling, twisted key from his capacious cloak and slipped it into a peculiarly shaped keyhole at the bottom of the door.

The door creaked open, and slow, sinuous light streamed through.

Lieutenant Patrick Brogan gasped at what lay on the other side.

CHAPTER 19

There were times in Jack Haldane's life as a cop at Demeter City when, all in all, he'd rather be back on the beat on the mean, but profoundly mundane, streets back home on Earth.

With a telekinetic kid in his arm, the kid's vomit splattered all over him, some strange alien energy being stalking him, the lights crashing out, and nascent panic clawing up from his gut, this was certainly one of them.

"The lights!" cried Jane Castle.

"Blatt!" said Yanx the Tarn baby.

"Damn!" said Jack.

Instinctively, he held the baby closer. Equally instinctively, Yanx held on to him, and for the first time Jack could feel his warmth and fear.

"Yo!" he cried to the people in the next room. "You want to give us principals back here some word on what the hell is going on?"

There was a pause, and the sound of frantic activity. Footsteps clomping, dials turning, chairs falling over, and other attendant confusion. Then there arose a humming sound, the comforting whir of electricity through circuitry and electronic gear.

"Sorry," someone finally said. "You okay back there?"

"Yeah. Only we can't *see* a whole lot."

"Just a moment. Stay where you are."

There didn't seem a whole lot of choice at the moment, and seeing that this place seemed about as safe as any other, and that Yanx seemed to be okay, Haldane figured that was actually just fine.

Yanx pressed himself close. The Tarn baby seemed to be shivering.

"You okay, Jane?"

"Yes."

"Look, I don't want to sound like I'm coming on, or I want us to get domestic or anything, but I've got a trembling kid here, and seeing as he's supposed to be getting protection from us, I guess a little comfort might help."

"What do you want me to do?"

"Let's start by you helping me to hold him."

"He's got you."

"Jane, really . . ."

"Blatt?" said Yanx querulously.

Somehow, this time "Blatt" sounded like "Please."

It broke Jane's hesitation. She came over and quietly pressed herself slightly against the baby.

Yanx sighed.

If he hadn't been feeling slightly panicked, Jack

himself might have enjoyed her touch. It did have a one-of-a-kind comfort to it, no question.

"He is trembling," said Jane. "There you go, Yanx. It'll be okay."

Even as they spoke, lights flickered tentatively back, then came on full.

A voice called from the next room.

"Why don't you-all come in here now?"

Jack recognized the voice. It was Rick, one of the security people. And it didn't sound particularly secure or confident.

"Okay. Let's go, little guy," said Jane. "You want me to take him, Jack?"

"Yeah. He seems to have stopped trembling."

It was true. And while Yanx wasn't exactly smiling and cooing with joy, Jack didn't sense the great fear, either.

He handed the baby over to Jane, and then led them all into the next room.

The people sitting around the machines of Security Central looked as though they could have used hugs as well. They were hunkered over their telltales, looking serious as Martian cancer.

"We've got a problem," said Rick.

"I noticed. What's happening?"

"We've got a bogey at the perimeter. And I don't mean the film star."

There was a haunted look in the security people's eyes that seemed to indicate it was more like "bogey" man, thought Haldane.

"Okay. Give it to us straight. Don't worry about the kid—he won't be able to understand."

"Good," said Rick. He brushed back a sweep of his long blond hair from his face. "Because it looks like whatever it was that came sniffing around that Tarn Arts Center and then dipped in for a Tarn baby snack is back, Jack."

"Ah."

"And this time it really means business."

"I'm braced. Give it to me."

"As you may recall, the whole idea of this operation was to snare the thing, somehow," said Parg the Creon. "The so-called Snare Crew was at the periphery." He tapped his communicator. "We're not getting anything out of them."

"Dead?"

"I hope not. In any case, what's important right now," said Rick, "is that they've been neutralized. Now it's that thing against us."

"Let me see."

Jack went up to the sensor scope.

The viewer gave a view of the building and the grounds from an over-top perspective. A slightly oscillating line indicated the perimeter force field fence that they were counting on to keep that strange thing out.

"What happened was this," said Rick, pointing at the quivering line. "That thing came from nowhere and just banged into the fence."

"It got through?" said Jane.

"I didn't say that," said Rick. "It just took a damned healthy bite out of our energy supply."

"You mean, it drained it?"

"Better believe it," countered Parg. "And it

pulled out our wiring to boot, to say nothing of communications. If we hadn't had the forethought to bring some self-generating units, we'd operating on candle power now."

"Well, I brought some candles, too," said Rick

The joke was met with cold silence.

"Sorry."

Parg took up the slack. "The good news is that there's no casualties in our ranks. We've still got the people, we've still got the firepower . . . And if that creature from the pits of damnation tries to get in here, you can bet we're just going to blow it back where it came from!"

"Comforting words," said Jack. "Question is, where's the thing now?"

"We're just trying to figure that out right now on the scope," said Rick. He tapped a button, then gestured Jack over.

"I'm playing back what we picked up during the attack. Watch."

Jack turned and looked at the schematic of the building overlaid on the surrounding area. At first all was calm and static. Suddenly, with a violent flash, there were lights screaming at the periphery.

Then the whole thing went black.

"What happened there?" asked Jane.

"Apparently," said Parg, "the thing just dropped from the sky. Impact, absorption—and, fortunately—expulsion."

"Or that's what it looks like, anyway," said Rick.

"You're saying this could be premeditated?" said Jack.

"Sure. Anything's possible. It could just be digesting its energy snack now . . . and biding its time to come down for the main meal."

"I love optimists," said Jane.

"You've got to be ready for anything."

Suddenly, an alarm went off.

Yanx began to cry.

A white burst of energy flowered on the screen.

"And the operative word in that phrase," whispered Jack Haldane, steeling himself, "is *'thing.'*"

CHAPTER 20

When she'd married her husband, Sally Brogan knew that there would be many nights and days when she'd be waiting for Patrick to come home, worried that something bad might have happened to him.

That was part of the bargain, and something that she'd been willing to accept as part of the bargain. It wasn't because she liked the idea a whole lot. It was because she loved Patrick and wanted to be with him and start a family with him.

However, when she'd signed on to be a cop's wife, nothing had prepared her for the kind of adventures she had here on Demeter City.

No, getting locked in a room by a nutty right-wing politician who'd just ordered some covert cohort to murder Patrick was not something she'd counted on.

Well it was no good dwelling on previous expectations.

Right now, it was necessary to deal with the

present moment—which still had a locked door in front of her.

"Damn!"

Normally, Sally Brogan didn't curse, but this seemed an appropriate time to make an exception to that rule. She tried the door once more just to be obsessive-compulsive about it and then stepped away, pacing back and forth to get rid of some of her excess energy and anxiety.

Thinking furiously.

There had to be some kind of way out of here. And if not, there had to be some kind of emergency call box or alarm. The trouble with the latter, however, was that use of same would alert her new enemies as to her presence here—

And they'd probably be able to figure out that she'd overheard certain pertinent information.

No, best to look for another way out.

She scoured the sides of the room, behind the stage and all around, but with no luck.

Then, suddenly, she remembered.

The women's room! It had a window!

She hurried back there, flung open the door, examined.

Yes, there it was. . . .

On the far end of the tiled room were two rectangular windows.

But where did they go?

She didn't remember which floor she was on, but it certainly wasn't the ground floor.

Well, there was nothing for it. She had to see what was on the other side of the windows.

They were not quite within her reach. She had to hurry back outside, snag a chair, and drag it back. Fortunately, however, the fasteners on the edge of the windows were not automatic and operable only from some faraway place. They were plain old fashioned hinge handles, and as manual as could be.

Alas, they were also slightly rusty and slightly stuck.

Again, Sally Brogan retreated to the adjacent room, hoping that no one would return and spot her. Fortunately, no one had returned, and Sally had time to cast about for a tool. A ransacking of the kitchen turned up a table knife, which would do in a pinch.

It took some force, but, with the right leverage, Sally pried open the latch. She was met by a blast of cold, wet air. She pushed the door all the way open. The sight that met her when she poked her head out was disconcerting, to say the least. The window opened to the outside. She was only seven floors up, but she'd be just as dead if she fell that distance to the street below as if she were seventy floors up. There was a ledge and the skeletal outline of an alien fire escape, with attendant metal ladder angling down into the rain and murky lights and splashing traffic.

There was also a mean wind whistling along the ledge that led to this fire escape.

Lovely.

She sighed. Fortunately, she was never one for fancy shoes, and she happened to be wearing ridged tennis shoes. She did not lose heart, but pulled herself through the window. She immediately shivered and felt a cold blast not just of wind, but of icy fear. Nonetheless, she kept on. Time was of the essence. Her husband's life depended on her actions—and her speed—now.

She crawled out and past the window, then stood up carefully. Using her hands to keep her steady, she made her way quickly and efficiently toward the strangely angled alien sculptured metal.

Reached for it—

Slipped.

Her shoe went out from under her with a suddenness that took her breath away. Fortunately, she was leaning in the right direction, and so her momentum carried her toward the metal structure.

As she fell, she grabbed hold of a length of coiling metal. It gave slightly, but held, giving her just enough time to grab it with her other hand before her other foot was dragged off.

Sally dangled for a moment over the sounds and smells of the city street. There was a moment of terror as she imagined herself hurtling into the maw of alien death . . .

Separated forever from those she loved.

However, her grip was firm, and the swing of her fall took her legs to the ladder. Instinctively, her legs wrapped around it, and clung. It took great patience and muscular control, but she managed to move over to the fire escape and plant her hands firmly on the ladder.

She took a deep breath, and then commenced her aching trip downward.

When, finally, she made it to the street, certain every centimeter of the way that the occasional light beam from a passing motorist was a spotlight focused on her descent, with the pleasure of hard firm ground below her she allowed herself the luxury of a heartfelt sigh.

She did not linger long in this position, but hurried to the nearest public comm unit.

She dialed the number that Patrick had given her to call if there was ever an emergency. She demanded to speak to Captain Podly. While she waited for her call to be rerouted, shivering under inadequate cover, she whispered an anxious mantra. "Hurry, Podly. Hurry."

Then the police captain's gruff voice came on.

"Captain Podly!" said Sally Brogan. "My husband's in terrible danger!"

CHAPTER 21

The thing was confused.

Its energies convulsed with contradictory impulses, a gridwork flux and wane of power.

However, above all, one passion ruled.

Hunger.

Even above the anger and frustration, and the flash/pulse of the charge that it had absorbed, it felt its instincts on fire.

It must consume.

Down below, it sensed its quarry, succulent and sweet, a power and a prey that, the thing knew, would somehow not only liberate it of its hunger, but its pain and confusion.

Now, as it poured a piercing arrow of itself through the shield that would keep it from its quarry, it rejoicing, ignoring the puny TinyEnergies that seemed to cluster around what it wanted.

Tonight it would feast.

Tonight it would know *what it truly was!*

CHAPTER 22

Patrick Brogan stared into the room with astonishment.

Just when he thought he'd seen the greatest wonders of the Universe, something else came along to top it.

He stood at the threshold of wonder and forever.

Beside him, Christina Fleur gasped.

Prismatic streamers of iridescence shot past in whirligigs of sensory explosions. Synesthesia of exotic senses rippled past his ears and nose and mouth, carrying a sting of something immortal and unattainable.

At first the overwhelming tumult of light blinded Brogan, but gradually his sight adjusted.

"Monk!" he said. "What *is* this?"

"It answers all your questions, I believe, Lieutenant Brogan," said the monk. "Please, look more closely."

Forms.

Shifting forms.

Shifting, lifting forms that wafted aglimmer on the floor, like ground fog variably frozen and aflutter.

Rainbow jaws seemed to open and shut, and as Brogan looked more closely he was able to see what lay on the floor, gushing light and dark, silent music and screaming quiet.

They appeared to be pieces of something connected by strands of gristle and cartilage, heaving in bloody silver, breathing with naked breastbones sticking up from pulsing organs.

"You're going to have to explain a little more than—"

"Sorry. No more explanations, Brogan. Your train through life stops at this station," Officer Fleur announced.

"Christina? What—"

He whirled around to see what this was all about—

—and found himself nose-to-muzzle with Officer Christina Fleur's gun.

"I'm sorry, Brogan," she said. "You're just getting a little too close for comfort. We have to deal with you in a manner befitting our cause."

"Cause?"

"He shall go to his demise with a question on his breath. A truly fitting manner of spiritual ascendence for a Seeker," said sausage-face.

A smirk crept over Christina's lovely features. "Nice working with you, partner."

She grabbed his gun.

Then, with a strong shove, she pushed him back . . .

. . . and then, with a swiftness that belied his bulk, the monk grabbed the door and slammed it.

Brogan hurled himself against the door, but to no avail.

It held fast.

He took a breath, and turned around to see what he faced.

Without the light from the adjacent chamber, Brogan could somehow better make out what lay on the floor. It was a clicking, moving mass, part biological and part . . . something else. As he stood there, staring at it, he was also aware that it was making a kind of scraping susurration.

His first impulse was that this must be some kind of hungry monster that would eat him as soon as it could. However, he could see neither mouth nor jaws nor claws.

Only a rippling mass of . . .

Something.

That something quivered and moved, and lights shot about.

The susurration grated again, and this time it sounded like some sort of words . . .

". . . hungry . . ." Brogan seemed to hear. "Hungry!"

These were *not* what the cop needed to hear about right now, not by a long shot.

"I mean no harm!" he said, just in case this thing—whatever it was—was capable of understanding.

The stuff on the floor clattered and shook. Clawed hands seemed to form. Structures resembling jaws with teeth of jewels formed from the mass, reared up, snapped at Brogan.

Brogan backed up.

But there was limited space in which to retreat before his back struck the closed door.

The very room seemed to vibrate with negative energy.

And Brogan recognized that energy.

It was the energy he felt when he was in a room of Tarns.

Powerful and intelligent mental energy.

The floor thing waved and flowed toward him. More and more it looked like some grisly torn apart beast of metal, silicon, and flesh, struggling to reassemble itself.

The room stank of hopelessness and desperation.

Slowly, it crawled toward him.

Brogan took a deep breath. He calmed himself, and willed his panic away. It was difficult, considering the circumstances. What was going on? His partner was a plant—but for whom . . . ?

These murders . . . They all circled this place . . . This *thing* . . . And yet also that energy being that threatened the Tarn baby . . .

All disparate elements that somehow didn't quite fall into a pattern. . . .

But what difference did it all make now, he thought as the wobbly organic substance flowed around his ankles. As the mucuslike liquid soaked his pants legs and he fancied he felt the sting of digestive juices, he nonetheless concentrated on keeping his calm. . . .

What was it that Took the Tarn had said to him once . . . ?

"All living beings can communicate mentally. Some have more power than others, but all have the potential. It all flows from a stillness of soul. . . . Pure consciousness, through which we all experience the Universe . . . We blend then. Perhaps we can experiment sometime, Patrick. But already I sense that a stronger mind than mine might communicate with you. . . ."

There was something here, something intelligent. . . . Brogan could sense that.

There was more here than hunger.

His only hope for survival now seemed to be create a stillness of mind that could fully allow this thing, whatever it was, to read his thoughts. . . .

If he was going to die, so be it. . . .

He surrendered himself to the nothingness of non-thinking. . . .

Only, from somewhere, deep in his own heart, he heard a voice that he recognized as his own deepest self.

Saying:

I mean no harm. I sense you need something. Do not harm me, and I know I can help you.

He opened himself to the thing's questing thoughts.

The flow of the stuff of the thing continued.

And the stinging began in earnest.

Like a breaking dam, he could feel the pain triumph and trigger the pure adrenaline of dread and fear.

For an awful moment he felt lost.

And then a thought that was not his bloomed in his head:

Tell me, Being. Where is my HALF?

CHAPTER 23

There were a lot of things that Jack Haldane didn't know. His pride occasionally gave way and admitted that.

However, there was one thing he would not admit:

That the "thing" was going to get this kid.

"Can it get in?" asked Jane. "Will the shield still hold it, even though they're on backup now?"

"That," said Rick, the human security technician, "is what we're about to find out." His voice was tense. Haldane could smell sweat in the air. "And very soon, to be perfectly honest."

"Soon" was an understatement.

The room shook.

Fixtures fell, clattering, to the floor.

The lights winked. The floor beneath them trembled.

Yanx took a momentary lull as an opportunity to start crying.

"I know how he feels," said Jane. "Isn't there anything we can do—anywhere we can run to?"

Jane wasn't exactly the running kind of person, but Jack knew exactly what she meant. This situation was fraught with a terror, a claustrophobic feeling pervading the horrifying immediacy of it all. Jack Haldane knew that if he wasn't a trained cop, and if he hadn't had plenty of experience with handling himself in emergency situations, he wasn't quite sure how he'd react now.

Probably, at the very least, sweat a lot.

Maybe he was doing that as well, but his most immediate concern was keeping that dreadful thing away from his charge.

"Is it holding?"

"I don't understand," said the security guy. "Our backups are even more powerful than the usual source. . . ."

"What's not to understand?" said Haldane, dreading the answer he knew would come back to him, judging from the sight he was seeing on the screen in front of him.

"Break out the weapons, people," said another, pulling his energy rifle out. "It's bashing through!"

Indeed, even as the man spoke, the white stuff that had been pushing in at the defensive perimeter schematic started moving inward. Simultaneously, explosions racked the building. Glass crashed and scattered. The floor rocked again.

Then, things were still again.

Preternaturally still.

Yanx stopped crying. The Tarn baby's eyes were

wide, and they went from side to side. It was as though he sensed the imminent arrival of the creature that had attempted to take him before. . . .

The five security personnel in the room were already hopping to action, pulling up various weapons in readiness.

"What's going on?" said Jack, grabbing up his own gun, unlatching the safety.

"Take a look yourself," said Parg.

Jack looked.

The rippling white that signified the creature was flowing past the perimeter like a tide of unfocused mist.

"It's going to be here in about twelve seconds," said Rick. "I strong suggest you take the kid and head here. . . ."

He tapped an area farthest away from the encroaching pool of energy. "It will buy you some more time. I'm sure reinforcements are on their way."

"No," said Jane. "Those guns aren't going to do a thing. If whatever psychic energy that Jack and I generate offends that thing, it can do just as good a job here as there."

"Jane's right. There's no reason to think we can't hold it off here, without abandoning you guys."

Parg shrugged. "We're here to protect the kid. That's our job."

All the others—humans, Tarns, and Creons alike—grunted and nodded in agreement.

Despite overwhelming feelings of impending doom, Jack Haldane could not help but feel a surge of solidarity with his companions—alien and human alike.

This was the future—all intelligent beings, working together to protect the innocent.

He'd have to write an article about it.

That was, if they could protect themselves and survive this dreadful onslaught of whatever was out there.

"We'll just have to protect the kid together," he said. "Jane, you and Yanx get behind me."

He noticed that Jane had her gun out as well. Yanx was looking at it as though he'd like to have one as well. Haldane didn't blame the little guy for that at all.

"How's it looking?" said Haldane, eyes directed toward the door.

"It's slowed down. It's like it's sniffing around first. Take a look for yourself."

Haldane looked down at the scanner. Sure enough, the white stuff flowing into the house was not traveling nearly as quickly as it had been before. Streamers flowed in like pseudopods of an amoeba, testing this room, testing that room.

Still, it wouldn't be long until some of that stuff got into the security room.

A terrible tension and apprehension filled the room.

"Jack," said Jane, holding the oddly silent Yanx close with one arm and her gun with the other. "Jack, if we get out of this alive . . . I tell you what . . ."

"What . . ."

"We'll have dinner, okay? Maybe a movie. You open doors for me and . . . and . . ."

"Look, Jane. You don't have . . ."

"I'll be nice to you the whole evening."

"Jane, you'd compromise your rigid virtue?"

She shot an alarmed look at him. "Hey! Not that nice!"

"Who ever said I'd compromise on mine?"

"Do we have to go to our possible deaths, bickering?"

"No. Let's go to our likely survival, bickering."

"Oh, the Power of Positive Thinking!"

"You do what you can. Take each moment as it comes and use it as a stepping-stone to the next, and in the immortal words of someone very near and dear to us—"

"Oh, Haldane, really. Aphorisms!"

"No! This is a good one! It's really very simple and to the point." Haldane cleared his throat, readying himself for the truism.

"Blatt!"

"Blatt?"

Yanx suddenly came alive. "Blatt! Blatt!" He pointed at Haldane as though to say, "Yes, by George, he's got it." "Blatt! Blatt!"

"Yes," said Haldane. "Be Likable and True, Totally."

"Blatt," said Jane Castle, thoughtfully. "Blatt. Be Less a Total Turkey!"

"No, no. Be Like a Terrific Toddler, Jane."

He gave her and Yanx a swift hug, and then looked toward the door.

One moment later, the energy thing rippled through.

CHAPTER 24

Somehow the thing seemed different than when Jack Haldane had seen it last.

Darker . . . edgier, now.

Ragged with jagged electricity.

Moiling, like oily clouds attempting to become clutching claws.

Jack Haldane didn't wait to try to bargain with it. He give it one beat to push some of its aethereal bulk through the doorway.

And then he fried it.

Or tried to, anyway. The energy bolt he sent at it slammed into it explosively, and there was a slight retreat . . . but all in all, it didn't seem to faze the thing very much at all.

"All together!" yelled Haldane. "Fire."

"Wait!" said Jane. "Is this going to do any good? I mean, if it absorbs energy . . ."

"Not exactly," said Rick. "It takes damage from direct electron overload. It's worth a try."

"Okay!" said Haldane. "Now!"

Weapons bristled. Nozzles directed toward the angry, wretched cloud that was moving in toward them.

Fired.

The thing lit from within, dancing a mottled contortion of spastic abandon.

Haldane fancied he heard it *scream* . . . and that was a satisfying sound indeed.

It started to move away.

Haldane had a thought. He quickly acted on it. He fired up at the top of the door. There was an explosion, and fiery bits of ceiling rained down upon the creature.

It moved back, and the wreckage from the ceiling cut off its progress into the room.

"Good job," said Parg. "Whatever else you've done, you've bought us a little time."

"Hope I don't have to pay for repairs," said Haldane.

"What about the comm line?" said Jane. "Can you get through to Took or anyone yet?"

Rick tried it again.

"No. But I'm sure they're on their way. As soon as that power outage happened, I'm sure they knew we were in deep trouble."

"I forgot . . . how long does it take to get from town to here?"

"About ten minutes."

Jack glanced at a chronometer. "That's about

five minutes from now. Think that wreckage is going to hold that creature that long?"

"I'm seeing what I can do with the generators," said Parg. "Maybe I can reroute . . ."

However, they received the answer to the question before they really wanted to.

"Look," said Jane. She raised her weapon, and not just to point.

There were chinks and cracks in the pile of supports and plaster and metal that had crashed down from the ceiling. Through these openings, separate sinuous smoky substances twirled, snaking out like ropes of spirit . . .

. . . and then twinging back together into an airborne pool of darkling, lightning shot something . . .

. . . and in this something, Jack thought he saw something like eyes, opening and staring at them. . . .

It must have been his imagination because the next moment the eyes were gone. However, the cloud was bigger, growing at an exponential rate and moving steadily toward them.

His gun went off, and the weapons of the others followed suit, blending into a chorus of fire and power.

However, this time they did not seem to deter the creature. Somehow, it just seemed to suck the firepower up, grow larger . . .

And progress.

"Jack! Jack! Help!"

Jane's voice.

Jack turned and saw that little Yanx was literally

being *pulled* from Jane's grasp, as though by some magnetic force. The Tarn baby stood out perpendicular from Jane, his eyes wide, his mouth open with astonishment and fright, no sounds emerging, a pleading in his face.

"Jack! Jack! What did we do last time?"

"I don't know!"

"Why isn't it working!"

Jack didn't answer, because he had to try something.

He stopped his stream of fire, and he grabbed hold of Yanx.

The baby looked as though he were trying to say something, but couldn't.

The cloud was large now, and a vortex opened up, like a maw into the bottom of darkness and nothingness.

Jack's arms began to ache with the strain of holding the kid back.

"Jack, Jack . . . concentrate . . . Think thoughts against the thing. Do what you did last time!"

In all truth, Jack Haldane couldn't say exactly *what* he'd done last time. Still, right now, he *could* concentrate.

He thought angry thoughts, thought power thoughts, thought all kinds of thoughts. He closed his eyes and he *willed* the creature away.

Fly he thought. *Shoo!*

Opened his eyes.

Felt himself being pulled, saw that vortexing max open wider.

And the smoke-ghost nearer.

"Jack!" screamed Jane.

And then the vortex clamped down on him and sucked him into its terrible emptiness.

CHAPTER 25

. . . flying . . .

. . . aloft, dangling from the claws of some monstrous bird of prey, the flap of gargantuan wings pounding against his body, the smell of a long distance to the ground . . .

. . . dangling . . .

. . . flying . . .

. . . darkness . . .

Jack Haldane felt streamers of sensation buffet him, wind and rain and the vacuum of space brushing against him violently, causing him to rock back and forth between consciousness . . .

. . . and unconsciousness . . .

. . . *"Jack,"* he heard a voice say in his ear.

And the rest was darkness.

◆ ◆ ◆

Jack felt as though someone had kicked him in the head, held him upside down, and then dumped him down some deep dark well. As he burbled up for breath, gasping, again his training and experience as a cop came into play, holding him back from tumbling the rest of the way into the chasm of pure panic.

He opened his eyes and established just what was going on. At first there was only gummy darkness, but as his eyes adjusted he saw that he lay on a rough flat surface, and beside him stretched the forms of both Jane Castle and Yanx. He was made aware of the cast on his arm, and renewed pain there. He'd hardly noticed it before, but now it throbbed.

Wind whistled, and he still had the giddy sensation of being at some great height. He looked up and saw that they seemed to be in some kind of gazebo-like room, opened to the vast night sky. Clouds rolled by, and all about he could see the exotic and alien skyline unique to Demeter City.

However, this view was entirely through some ectoplasmic scrim, vibrating and cracked with shimmering electric current.

The Energy-Creature!

But why were they still alive?

He shook Jane's shoulder. "Jane. Wake up!"

She came to almost immediately, blink and gasping. "What? How—"

"It's okay. We're alive. It hasn't killed us," said Jack. "Looks like it's taken us to some sort of . . . of *aerie*. Atop a skyscraper."

"Skyscraper . . ." she said. Jack could feel her shudder. "Damn. Yanx . . ."

They both reached down and touched the Tarn baby. He was breathing deeply and regularly, in peaceful, restful sleep. A sigh, a squirm, and that was all.

"Well, he seems to be all right."

"Yes, but what about the long run?" Jane got up, looking around, just short of frantic. She reached to her holster for her gun, came up empty. "I mean, yes it seems to be on the skyline, but *where* on the skyline? And how do we get down?"

She reached again to her belt. There was nothing there. "My comm. That's gone, too."

Jack had already determined that he, too, had lost all of his weapons, as well as his radio. And he'd begun to cast about for the way down.

He found it.

"There."

Without rising or causing overmuch attention, he scooted over to the center of the skyscraper top. There was some kind of handle there, and as soon as he reached it he was able to see by the outlines and ridges that the handle was attached to the door. He pulled at that handle, but it held fast.

"Damn. It's locked."

"And there's no other way down?"

"You want to go over there and check for a ladder?"

Jane looked up. She gasped as, for the first time apparently, it registered on her that all sides of the building top were covered by the energy membrane of the creature that had apparently carried them here.

"Oh shit."

"Oh yes. You see why I'm astonished that we're still alive. Where there's life, there's hope, I guess . . . but I sure would like to know why that thing's keeping us alive. . . ."

"And what it wants!" said Jane, shaking her head sorrowfully.

"It's very confused," said a small, precise voice. "It needs help. But it's also hungry. We must consider that."

"Who said that?" Brogan looked around.

"Who's there?" said Jane, equally astonished.

"Me," said the voice again, and Jack looked down.

Sitting up was Yanx the Tarn baby.

"Yanx?" he said, disbelievingly.

"None other, Jack Haldane. My goodness, I feel much more at home sitting, but I suppose I should stand and thank you formally for your devotion and friendship. I realize that I've been quite the ordeal."

The Tarn baby got up and offered his little hand.

Stunned, Jack Haldane took it, shook it.

"Yanx? You're *speaking*?" said Jane. "How?"

The baby turned and offered its hand to her. "Hello, Jane Castle. I thank you, too, for your affection and concern. We appear to be in quite the pickle!"

Jane took the hand shook it.

"I don't understand. . . ."

"No. I am aware of the fact that this taking on of personality, advanced intelligence, to say nothing of voice, is quite shocking to you." The Tarn baby stepped closer to them, and Jack Haldane could now see very clearly that the eye in the middle of its forehead was wide-open, peering up at them quizzically.

"To say the least," said Jane.

"You bet, kid. Maybe you'd better explain . . . you mean all that time you were acting like a baby, you were pulling our legs!"

"Absolutely not! I quite assure you, my behavior was quite typical for a rambunctious intelligent Tarn infant of my age. Indeed, that would still be my consciousness and mental age level now—if not for something very significant."

"Look, we might be killed any moment," said Jack. "I'd rather not go to my death in total suspense!"

Yanx sighed. "You forget. I am not a human infant. I am a Tarn infant. Over the millennia of development, our race has developed peculiar and singular methodologies for survival, involving our mental powers. For, you see, those mental powers are much more complex than lifting things telekinetically and reading minds. I will not take the time to attend to complexities. Suffice it to say that in times of stress and continual threat, a portion of a Tarn infant's brain is empowered to advance temporarily and tap into the racial and intelligence memory planted there at its birth. This allows it, for hours at a time, to develop speech, motor control, and other aspects of adult abilities and behavior in order to deal with threats to its well-being."

"Amazing!" said Jane. "But why didn't Took tell us about this? Warn us what we might have to expect."

The Tarn baby shook its head. "This ability is a guarded secret among our kind. For instance, no Creon is aware of this ability. . . . So we have to ask for your silence on the subject in the future."

"If we have a future!" said Jack.

"Yanx . . . If your intelligence has increased . . . then so have your mental powers?" said Jane.

"Oh indeed. And I believe I have an answer and a course of action that we might take, with my facilitation."

"Well, don't wait until you're burbling again," said Jack. "Clue us in."

"This creature . . . indeed it is hungry, and it would consume our energies."

"Yes. But why is it after *you*, especially?" asked Jack.

"An excellent question! And I have pondered that as well," said Yanx. "According to the perceptions of my mental abilities and simple deduction, I should say that my energy is of an intense and specialized nature. . . . Also, I perceive that somehow the thing is somehow incomplete . . . and somehow strives toward that final fulfilling completion . . . the exact nature of which, of course, I cannot hazard at this point. However, above all, I detected a fierce hunger and thirst for our energies in the being."

"Oh, that's just peachy-keen. We're going to be Energy Sodas for the thing after all!"

"Jack. Shut up and let Yanx talk," scolded Jane.

"Communication is impossible at this point; however, I am able to read it sufficiently to distinguish the dilemma," said Yanx. "This is an intelligent being, not of our planet. It is lost and confused. It hungers for that which would replenish its energies . . . but it also desperately seeks something else . . ."

"Why didn't it just suck the energy out of us like it did with the other beings?"

"You forget. It was the mental energy interplay between the two of you, that originally—"

Suddenly, a creaking sounded.

Jack spun around in time to see the door in the middle of the open room push open. . . .

A head stuck through, and Jack Haldane recognized it instantly.

"Brogan!"

CHAPTER 26

"Lieutenant Brogan!" said Jane Castle.

"Oh! Excellent!" said Yanx the Tarn baby. "A savior!"

Patrick Brogan blinked. "Look, I've had a hard enough day. . . . You want to tell me what's going on here—"

"Yes, I'd be happy to explain," said Yanx. "You see—"

"Look," said Brogan. "Let me just take it for granted and get it all in the wrap up, okay? No one was hurt back at your so-called Safe Quarters. The thing merely snatched you. Must not have been quite able to digest you. I understand you were quite a sight, the three of you floating through the moonlit sky, encased in an Energy Creature. Right now, there's this energy being out there, and it still seems to be erring on the wrong side of malevolence. I've got a few ideas I'd like to work with, and I've brought a few assistants. So right now I'd like to start implementing them." He turned around and yelled down the stairway. "Okay, Podly. Bring up our guests."

He stepped up onto the top, getting out of the way of the new arrivals.

"All right then," came the surly, cranky voice of his captain. "Move lively then . . . and remember. There's a shaky finger behind this gun here. And we Creon policemen are a wee bit tetchy when we're dealing with conniving *kackva* imbibers like your lot."

The Ardentian monk came first. Kawkor. Sausage-face. Silent but face ashake.

Then Officer Christina Fleur, staring beautiful daggers at him at first, but then suddenly contrite as she stepped up and saw the billowing wonder that was the Energy-Creature, draped over the top of the high building.

And, finally, none other than Joseph Salamander.

It hadn't been difficult to pick them up.

Kawkor, the monk in the temple, had been conferring with Salamander at the temple itself, doubtless thinking that Patrick Brogan was falling victim to their Half-a-Creature in the dungeon. In fact, Podly had taken them, even before he'd found out where Brogan was and opened the door for him. All thanks to his dear brave wife, bless her heart.

Salamander was blustering as usual. "You can't do this to me! I am an emissary of the United States government!"

Podly himself stepped up, followed by three other members of Demeter City's Finest.

"Yes, but you're in *my* city now, and it would seem that you've been up to some serious mischief. And not only are we going to push your nose in it a bit, you're going to help solve the little problem we have, right."

"I can't do anything. . . . This guy here . . . he controls the thing," said Salamander. "In fact—" But the sight of the sparkling Energy-Creature shut him up. "Jeez . . . it's *huge.*"

"I believe that 'control' is the wrong term," said the monk. "I do not know why you have brought us here. There is nothing that *we* can do."

"Oh, I think that there's *a lot* that you can do, Mr. Monk," said Brogan. "First off, you can alert this poor thing that its better half is waiting to reunite with it, below."

"Wait a minute. What the hell are you talking about?" said Haldane. "Would you care to clue us in as to what's been going on?"

"That *would* be nice," said Jane.

"Oh, *super*," said Yanx. "Below? This may work out very well indeed!"

Brogan said, "I pretty much found out where our Energy-Creature came from . . . and what it is, and why it's doing what it's doing." He took a breath, thought for a moment, then painted a brief sketch. "These monks had it captured and smuggled from a far-distant planet, at the behest of what appears to be a massive galactic conspiracy of a government party from Earth to achieve human supremacy in the Universe."

"Wow," said Jack. "We're going from macro to mega here!"

"It's a creature called the Vibrost, a symbiont/host relationship between two separate species—one planet bound, the other a half-energy, half-matter creature. The species have evolved to the point where the two are separable . . . but they revert to bestial nature and are confused and damaged. How the monks knew of this, I don't know. . . . Maybe they used one before, on some other planet, to create this kind of effect?"

"Effect?" said Jane.

"Yes. The Mad Hungry God-Thing on the Loose. Very good for religious purposes, I take it. Alas, it's not the most easily guided God-Thing in the Universe . . . but it does strike terror into hearts, and fear like that is just the sort of thing that cults such as these thrive on, hmmm?"

"You are disgustingly ignorant of the intricacies of our theology," said the monk, sniffing imperiously.

"Be that as it may, the formula was working . . . only what Salamander here needed was a dreadful alien being to terrify the human populace . . . and have *proof* that this was a stark and dangerous Universe out here, and all mankind should conquer first and ask intricate theological questions later."

"Nonsense. I am innocent of all this!" said Salamander.

"Ah! I think not!" said Podly. "I've had a private little talk with Ms. Fleur here, and the darling sang like the gilded *klinzo* bird." Podly's eyebrows waggled. "And from what I hear, you're not only going to have a lot of explaining to do to your constituency . . . you've got a lot of explaining to do to your wife."

"I'm afraid that once all this gets into the Earth news media," said Brogan, "your backward-looking party is going to take a slight tumble in the polls. . . . And alas, also at the voting booths."

"You bitch!" snarled the politician, accelerating from defeat to active rage in an inkling.

One of the officers had strayed too close to him. With a power and a violence that he'd not looked capable of, the politician stepped forward, yanked a spare gun from the Creon's holster, switched off the safety, and blasted his confederate.

Christina Fleur screamed and went down.

It all happened so quickly that Brogan barely had time to swing his own gun over toward Salamander.

When it got there, it was too late.

"Don't move!" said Salamander. "Move and I'll kill you all!"

"Don't be stupid, Salamander," said Brogan. "You'll not get anywhere."

"Oh no? We'll see about that! You don't know what kind of power I have here on Demeter City, Brogan. . . . And whatever power I have here, I have *much* more, back home on Earth. The destiny of mankind is domination. Let me give you a little taste of domination! Now get out of the way and let me out of here. I've got places to go and things to—"

It happened so quickly Matthew Brogan was

barely able to register it. One moment, Salamander was standing there, holding a gun aimed at the group . . .

. . . and the next a milky, shining tentacle of force whipped around him, knocking the weapon from his hand. It clanked and skittered on the floor.

Salamander screamed.

He was yanked off his feet . . .

And then slowly carried out the window of the building. Writhing and screaming, he was carried into the milky mass of the Energy-Creature . . .

"Help me! Help me!" he cried. "Don't let it eat me! Help me . . ."

Abruptly, though, the politician was let go, and with a shrill shriek that lasted for a terribly long time, he fell a skyscraper's length to the pavement below.

The Energy-Creature, rippled and quivered, without comment.

"Looks like Republicans weren't to our Floating Energy Alien's taste," said Brogan.

"And Officer Fleur?"

"Unconscious," said Podly. "But she'll be all right. If we can get her down."

"Do it. I need to somehow tell this thing that it's got something waiting down on the street for it," said Brogan. "This seems to be its hangout, and it might take some talking to get it down so it can make the connection, so we can have an intelligent alien to deal with, and not two confused things in pain and disarray."

"Actually, Lieutenant," said Yanx, "I have just

been communicating with it, and transferred the information. It is taking a few moments to digest the information, but it appears to be reacting in a favorable manner."

"Okay," said Brogan. "You can tell me now. Since when can a baby talk?"

"We'll explain later," said Jack. "For now, let's just call it a Tarn survival trait."

"Communicating with it—" said Jane. "Yanx, that's wonderful. Are you sure it's—"

Yanx's expression changed suddenly. The third eye fluttered, and the smile turned to a frown.

"Oh dear."

Even as he said the words, the stuff of the Energy-Creature began to flow through to the aerie's . . ."

"No," said Yanx. "Lieutenant Brogan. Quickly! It misunderstands! He thinks it's below our feet. Hurry and visualize its location—"

Brogan took a breath. Another instance of panic control. However, knowing that he had done it before successfully was of great help. His communications with the strong mental powers of the creature in the dungeon had been primitive and simple, to say the least . . . but they'd been effective enough.

He calmed himself.

At the Vibrost's behest, they had somehow helped to load it into a van large enough to accommodate it. It was down there, below, in that van. Were its psychic emanations insufficient to attract its Half? That must be the case, although it did little good to ponder such.

Now he had to concentrate on the image.

There it was: the van. And inside—he visualized his memory of the shattered-looking creature.

And then he felt the frizzing, electric touch of the cloud thing on his face . . .

"Yes," he heard Yanx say. "Yes. Down. Far below!"

Brogan felt immense power, barely held in check . . . crackling and mixing before him in turmoil . . .

And then it lessened.

He opened his eyes in time to see it withdraw. Coalesce. With a quickening speed, it lowered itself.

Was gone.

He breathed a sigh of relief.

"Well then," said Yanx. "I can't speak for the rest of you, but I'd like to get down from here. It's *way* past my bedtime!"

EPILOGUE

If Jack Haldane had been a drinking man, this would be a six-pack plus kind of evening.

However, at this point even champagne with Jane Castle was not a particularly welcome thought. He felt drained and tired. Nonetheless, he well knew the value of debriefing after some serious stress. It kind of got things off the chest as well as the mind, and it would allow him to rest a hell of a lot better tonight.

The debriefing point this evening was the precinct house, and they all sat in front of Podly's desk now, sipping their favorite late-evening relaxing potions of a nonalcoholic nature.

Jack was working on an alien drink he was partial to because it tasted rather like his favorite drink back home: Yoo Hoos.

In attendance were Lieutenant Brogan, and wife (who sat lovingly close, and no wonder—Mrs. B.

had certainly helped them out today), some of the security people from the house (none of whom had been killed, fortunately), Jane Castle . . . and the still quite intelligent and vocal Yanx, who somehow hadn't gotten around to his bedtime. Beside him sat Took.

"I certainly am happy that my parents will be all right," said Yanx. "Although I should like to ask you that you not mention that I was forced to develop quickly for a time. It's very hard for parents to think of their child as more than a sweet, cooing baby." He blinked. "Indeed, it's very hard for me as well. It has been a bit of a strain."

"Well, you can be sure your secret will stay safe with us," said Podly. "An amazing survival characteristic, I must say. It makes me even more respectful of the Tarn race than before."

"That's good to know," said Took.

"It's nice to see two different species getting along and cooperating so well," said Sally Brogan. "Believe me, I am truly ashamed that the human race produced men like Salamander and his ilk."

"You can be sure that we'll do our very best to see that this political party loses it bite back on Earth," said Brogan.

"A few choice interviews hither and yon would seem to be very much in order," said Jane Castle. "And with Officer Fleur out of danger now, I'm sure she'll want to do as much as possible to reduce her jail sentence."

"It's going to be a long, hard slog against that kind of poisonous political attitude," said Brogan.

"But that's what we're working for . . . and what we're instilling in our own children."

"Understanding and compassion, yes," said Sally. "I'm so happy that the Vibrost is mending as well."

"Yes, the Bonding was extremely stressful, but necessary," said Yanx. "But it is resting comfortably now."

"And in a safe place," said Podly. "We're arranging for its return to its homeworld . . . and taking precautions that this kind of thing never happens again." With great satisfaction, he punched a few keys on his console. "Case more or less closed." He sighed and shook his big head. "So, Yanx. How long will we have the pleasure of your company in this form?"

"Blatt!" said Yanx.

"Pardon?"

"Blatt!"

The Tarn baby gurgled and smiled. Then it yawned with great self-satisfaction.

"I think that Advanced Yanx just hit bedtime," said Jack.

"I hope we get to know him more when he gets to that stage normally!" said Jane. "Quite a fine fellow."

"And you two," said Took. "You were absolutely wonderful with him. In my opinion, you're going to make just terrific parents!"

Jane Castle blushed. "Took!"

"Hey! We haven't even had our first date together yet!" said Jack. "But you know, come to think of it . . . a kid with my looks and your brains . . ."

"But supposing this hypothetical child has my looks and *your* brains?" Jane shook her head mournfully. "Disaster!"

"Jane! You know, after all we've been through, you could give me a compliment!"

"Oh, the torture continues . . ." said Jane.

Jack looked away. Somehow, he felt terribly weary, and his normal defenses weren't up. This time her mocking words . . . as well as her tone . . . smarted.

He sighed.

"Yanx!"

He turned, and was confronted by the sight of Jane Castle, floating in the air in front of him.

"Yanx! Put her down!"

Yanx giggled.

Jane slowly settled down from her telekinetic ride into Jack Haldane's lap.

"Blatt!" said Yanx. "Blatt!"

Jane sighed. "Just what does that mean, anyway, Yanx?"

Jack was happy that Jane was making no immediate attempt to get off his lap. She felt very . . . well, nice.

"Blatt," said Yanx again.

Immediately, the baby turned and planted a wet one on Took's lips.

"Oh my," said Took. "Well, the child doesn't seem to have totally devolved."

"Blatt!" said Brogan. "I rather like the concept." He leaned over and softly kissed his wife.

Podly was looking rather baffled.

Jane's lips were pursed. She looked at Jack, and Jack looked at her.

She raised an eyebrow.

"Well, I don't suppose it would hurt to do it once You have been rather the hero, haven't you."

And she leaned her lips toward his.

Afterward, "Blatt" was Jack Haldane's absolutely favorite word in the whole Universe.

Slomo, the precinct robot, watched this osculatory display between Jane Castle and Jack Haldane with vast vexation.

"It appears that I will soon have to pay you your one hundred credits, Orrinn," said the metal being, its lights blinking in a particularly complex and confused fashion.

"Disgusting!" said the orange-haired Creon. "Mouth. Doubtless tongue to tongue! We Creons know the proper use of tongues!" He nodded to himself with great satisfaction. "I don't know, Slomo. See! It is a very short physical contact! And look, she is already off his lap." He shook his head. "I would take your hundred credits. However, I strongly suspect I would soon have to hand it back!"

Slomo's cortex department craned up, then sat suddenly back down. He swiveled his oculars toward Orrinn, bemused.

"I shall never understand human beings," said the robot. "I think perhaps they are the strangest of the aliens in this new alien Universe."

Orrinn nodded. "Indeed! Have you seen any of their television programs! Truly bizarre!" The Creon draped a friendly arm around his metallic friend. "It is good to be normal, is it not?"

His tongue slipped out and touched the robot's head case.

Slomo stepped back, stunned.

"What have you done?"

"That? Just a friendly lick! An honored Creon custom."

"Ah. An interesting sensation."

Slomo the robot looked over at the two young humans, sitting together and smiling at each other as the heated conversation among the group in the precinct station continued.

"Orrinn."

"Yes, Slomo."

"If I had a tongue . . . I think I should like to lick Officer Castle."

Orrinn looked over to where Officer Castle sat, looking bright and perky despite all her recent adventures.

Not enough warts, and the skin was far too smooth . . .

And far, far too skinny.

But all in all, he supposed some things did translate from planet to planet. Things like spunk, spirit, and character . . .

In fact, all these humans had these qualities.

Orrinn suddenly felt very good indeed.

"Slomo. I've made a momentous decision!"

"Yes, Orrinn!"

"A hundred credits is small change! We'll make a million credits. Together, we will write a best-selling nonfiction book: *The Mating Habits of Human Beings*. Volume One of a series: *Mondo Homo Sapiens!*"

Slomo the robot liked the idea very much.

The newest imprint of
HarperPaperbacks
presents the hottest
new writers and
the classics!

HarperPrism

THE BEST IN SCIENCE FICTION & FANTASY...

Isaac **Asimov**........................
........................C.J. **Cherryh**
Ursula K. **Le Guin**.................
..................Robert **Gleason**
Terry **Pratchett**......................
..............Kathlyn **Starbuck**
Tad **Williams**.........................
......................Gahan **Wilson**
Janny **Wurts**...........................
.........................The **X**-Files™
Magic: The Gathering™......
..The **World** of **Darkness**™

TODAY... AND TOMORROW

PR-003

HarperPrism
An Imprint of HarperPaperbacks

IT'S MAGIC The Gathering™

FREE CARD OFFER WITH BOOKS #1-#4!

#1 ARENA by William R. Forstchen

#2 WHISPERING WOODS by Clayton Emery

#3 SHATTERED CHAINS by Clayton Emery

#4 FINAL SACRIFICE by Clayton Emery

 # 5 THE CURSED LAND by Teri McLaren (September 1995)

 # 6 THE PRODIGAL SORCERER by Mark Sumner (November 1995)

Visa & Mastercard holders—for fastest service call 1-800-331-3761

MAIL TO: HarperCollins*Publishers*
P.O. Box 588 Dunmore, PA 18512-0588

- ❑ **Arena** 105424-0 .... $4.99 U.S. /$5.99 CAN.
- ❑ **Whispering Woods** 105418-6 .... $4.99 U.S. /$5.99 CAN.
- ❑ **Shattered Chains** 105419-4 .... $4.99 U.S. /$5.99 CAN.
- ❑ **Final Sacrifice** 105420-8 .... $4.99 U.S. /$5.99 CAN.
- ❑ **The Cursed Land** 105016-4 .... $4.99 U.S. /$5.99 CAN.
- ❑ **The Prodigal Sorcerer** 105476-3 ..... $5.50 U.S. /$6.50 CAN.

Subtotal .... $________
Postage and Handling .... $ 2.00
Sales Tax (Add applicable sales tax) .... $________
Total .... $________

Name________________
Address________________
City________________
State________ Zip________

Remit in U.S. funds. Do not send cash. Allow up to 6 weeks for delivery.
(Valid only in U.S. & Canada.) Prices subject to change. P010

Magic: The Gathering™ is a trademark of Wizards of the Coast, Inc.

ENTER THE WORLD OF DARKNESS™

SUCH PAIN

◆

NETHERWORLD

◆

WYRM WOLF

◆

DARK PRINCE

◆

CONSPICUOUS CONSUMPTION*

◆

SINS OF THE FATHERS*

***coming soon**

The World of Darkness™ is a trademark of the White Wolf Game Studio.

From HarperPrism

MAIL TO: **HarperCollins Publishers**
P.O. Box 588 Dunmore, PA 18512-0588
OR CALL: (800) 331-3761

Yes, please send me the books I have checked:

❑ **SUCH PAIN** 105463-1	$4.99 U.S./ $5.99 CAN.
❑ **WYRM WOLF** 105439-9	$4.99 U.S./ $5.99 CAN.
❑ **NETHERWORLD** 105473-9	$4.99 U.S./ $5.99 CAN.
❑ **DARK PRINCE** 105422-4	$4.99 U.S./ $5.99 CAN.
❑ **CONSPICUOUS CONSUMPTION** 105471-2	$4.99 U.S./ $5.99 CAN.
❑ **SINS OF THE FATHERS** 105472-0	$4.99 U.S./ $5.99 CAN.
SUBTOTAL	$________
POSTAGE AND HANDLING	$2.00
SALES TAX (Add applicable sales tax).	$________

Name____________________

Address____________________

City__________ State______ Zip______

Allow up to 6 weeks for delivery. Remit in U.S. funds. Do not send cash.
(Valid in U.S. & Canada.) Prices subject to change. P008

$1,000.00

FOR YOUR THOUGHTS

Let us know what you think. Just answer these seven questions and you could win $1,000! For completing and returning this survey, you'll be entered into a drawing to win a $1,000 prize.

OFFICIAL RULES: *No additional purchase necessary.* Complete the HarperPaperbacks questionnaire–be sure to include your name and address–and mail it, with first-class postage, to HarperPaperbacks, Survey Sweeps, 10 E. 53rd Street, New York, NY 10022. Entries must be received no later than midnight, October 4, 1995. One winner will be chosen at random from the completed readership surveys received by HarperPaperbacks. A random drawing will take place in the offices of HarperPaperbacks on or about October 16, 1995. The odds of winning are determined by the number of entries received. If you are the winner, you will be notified by certified mail how to collect the $1,000 and will be required to sign an affidavit of eligibility within 21 days of notification. A $1,000 money order will be given to the *sole winner* only–to be sent by registered mail. Payment of any taxes imposed on the prize winner will be the sole responsibility of the winner. All federal, state, and local laws apply. Void where prohibited by law. The prize is not transferable. **No photocopied entries.**

Entrants are responsible for mailing the completed readership survey to HarperPaperbacks, Survey Sweeps, at 10 E. 53rd Street, New York, NY 10022. If you wish to send a survey without entering the sweepstakes drawing, simply leave the name/address section blank. Surveys without name and address will not be entered in the sweepstakes drawing. HarperPaperbacks is not responsible for lost or misdirected mail. Photocopied submissions will be disqualified. Entrants must be at least 18 years of age and U.S. citizens. All information supplied is subject to verification. Employees, and their immediate family, of HarperCollins*Publishers* are not eligible. For winner information, send a stamped, self-addressed №10 envelope by November 10, 1995 to HarperPaperbacks, Sweeps Winners, 10 E. 53rd Street, New York, NY 10022.

HarperPaperbacks

would like to give you a chance to win $1,000.00
and all you have to do is answer these easy questions.

Please refer to the previous page for official rules and regulations.

Name: ______________________ Sex: M 01 F 02

Address: ______________________

City: ______________ State: ________ Zip: ________

Age: 7-12 03 13-17 04 18-24 05 25-34 06 35-49 07 50+ 08

We hope you enjoyed reading ***Demon Wing***

1 a) Did you intend to purchase this particular book? Y 09 N 10
b) Was this an impulse purchase? Y 11 N 12

2) How important were the following in your purchase of this book?
(1 = not important; 3 = moderately important; 5 = very important)

word of mouth	1 13	3 14	5 15	advertising	1 31	3 32	5 33
cover art & design	1 16	3 17	5 18	plot description	1 34	3 35	5 36
cover glitz	1 19	3 20	5 21	price	1 37	3 38	5 39
cover color	1 22	3 23	5 24	author	1 40	3 41	5 42
floor stand/display	1 25	3 26	5 27	length of book	1 43	3 44	5 45
contest offer	1 28	3 29	5 30				

3) In general, how do you find out about the books you want to read?

____ 46 word of mouth
____ 47 book reviews
____ 48 libraries
____ 49 store browsing
____ 50 author publicity
____ 51 reader's clubs
____ 52 advertising

4) Where did you buy this book?

Store Name: ______________________

City/State: ______________________

5) Have you ever listened to a book on tape? Y 53 N 54

6) How many of the following do you buy each month?

mass market paperbacks	0 55	1-2 56	3-5 57	5+ 58
large format paperbacks	0 59	1-2 60	3-5 61	5+ 62
hardcovers	0 63	1-2 64	3-5 65	5+ 66
spoken audio products/books on tape	0 67	1-2 68	3-5 69	5+ 70

7) What types of books do you usually buy? (check all that apply)

____ 71 mystery/suspense/thriller
____ 72 science fiction/fantasy/horror
____ 73 true crime
____ 74 westerns
____ 75 reference
____ 76 business
____ 77 romance/women's fiction
____ 78 self-help/inspirational
____ 79 entertainment/Hollywood
____ 80 young adult (age 13+)
____ 81 children's (ages 7-12)
____ 82 nonfiction/other

please return to:
HarperPaperbacks, Survey Sweeps, 10 East 53rd Street, New York, NY 10022